HOUR OF THE HORDE

As a horde of monstrous travelers advances through space annihilating everything before it, a super-defense force, consisting of one especially talented man from each as yet untouched planet, converges in an attempt to turn back the horde.

Miles Vander, Earth's representative, finds himself with a small group regarded as the less "civilized" of the defending force. But in the final showdown, it is these creatures capable of independent action and raw courage who give a surprising twist to this galactic cliffhanger . . .

ALSO BY GORDON DICKSON

SPACEPAW

GORDON DICKSON
HOUR OF THE HORDE

A BERKLEY MEDALLION BOOK
PUBLISHED BY
BERKLEY PUBLISHING CORPORATION

BERKLEY MEDALLION EDITION, FEBRUARY, 1971

SBN 425-01957-8

BERKLEY MEDALLION BOOKS are published by Berkley Publishing Corporation 200 Madison Avenue New York, N. Y. 10016

BERKLEY MEDALLION BOOKS ® TM 757,375

Printed in the United States of America

1

It had happened again. That primitive, unconquerable power in him that he could not seem to deny had reached out once more, savagely, down the muscles of his good arm and hand, to take over his painting.

Exhausted, Miles Vander threw the number four brush he held, now bloodily tipped with alizarine red, back into the pint fruit jar of muddy turpentine holding the other long, yellow-handled brushes. A feeling of dull exhaustion and frustration dropped on him like the doubled folds of some heavy blanket.

All at once he was aware again of his own starved-looking body, his bent shoulders, his uselessly hanging left arm that polio had crippled six years ago. The paralyzed hand was now tucked into his left pants' pocket, out of sight, and the loose sleeve of his white shirt, billowing about the wasted arm in the late sunlight of the warm spring afternoon, disguised for the moment its unnatural thinness. But he was suddenly, grimly, once more aware of it just the same.

For a few hours, caught up in his painting, he had forgotten both his crippling and the stubborn artistic search he had never stopped these last five years. Now emptied and worn-out, he stood with the aftertaste of one more failure, staring at his canvas, as the freshening breeze of the late afternoon blew the white shirt coldly about him, molding it to his cooling body.

The painting showed the scene before him—only, it did not. He stood on the parkway grass above the west bluff over the Mississippi River. Rippleless below him, between high rock walls narrowly footed with green park lawn, the three-hundred-yard width of the upper river flowed darkly blue, with picture-postcard calmness, beneath the white concrete of a freeway bridge bearing a glassed-in overhead walkway for students moving between the east and west campuses of the university.

These things made up the landscape he had been painting for three and a half hours. And he had set them all down on canvas—the tall gray-brown river bluffs, the

5

grass-covered flats at the foot of the bluffs, even the white-paddle-wheeled steamboat that was the university's theater-on-the-river moored below the bridge. He gazed at them now, and at the large, heavily leaved old elm trees, the reddish-brown brick of the student union and the university hospital on top of the far bluff, and the blue, near-cloudless sky above them all.

These things lay, as they had lain all through the hours of his painting, bathed in the gentle sunlight of late May—making a warm, even comforting, scene. But this was not the way his brushes had reproduced them on canvas.

On the now wetly gleaming, color-laden three-by-four-foot square of cloth he had painted not what he faced, but that old savage animal instinct of man to which he could not seem to close his eyes—ever. Into the soft, living greens and blues and browns of the scene across the river had crept the icy bleakness of oil-based ultramarine blue hardened with gray. Into the soft yellow sunlight had come the smouldering fire of alizarine red, raising a sullen reddishness like the color of spilled blood.

The resulting painting showed the works of man, by which man was himself to be judged, grayed and brooding, stripped down, and hardened and stained with the bloody marks of savage guilts and primitive failures.

Miles felt exhausted, weak—even a little dizzy. He had emptied himself once more of his inner creative energy. But once more he had made—not the image of the world he wished to show, but only that image's other face; like the other side of a coin, its devil face. Wearily he began cleaning his brushes and packing his paints for the return to his room.

Midway across the glassed-in walkway above the free-way bridge he stopped to rest for a minute, propping his now-covered canvas and heavy paint box upon the railing that protected the glass side of the walkway. While he caught his breath, he stared down once more at the scene of his painting.

Back the way he had come was the top of the bluff on which he had set up his easel, and facing him now was the bluff's rugged, near-vertical face of gray limestone rock, roughened, cracked, and gullied by weather, standing above the lower strip of parkway greensward at its foot. As always, the sight of that bluff-face pumped new strength and purpose into him. What he had done once, he could do again. A little warmth woke in him again.

He had been defeated once more this afternoon, but not conquered, after all. Already, drawing strength from the sight of the gray-brown cliff face, the thoughts began to kindle of the next time he would put brush to canvas. There was still time for him to succeed. After all, if he was a failure, at least he was a failure, so far, only in his own eyes.

His painting, even as it was, had won him the unusual attention of his instructors at the university school of art. It had also won him, now that he was graduating, a grant which would let him spend the next two years in Europe, moving about and painting as he liked. Then free at last from academic distractions, painting, painting, and continually painting, he would finally win out over that savage, primitive bleakness of viewpoint which seemed determined to express itself in everything he did.

The slight dizziness from the long afternoon's effort made him giddy again for a moment. He leaned against the railing. But then he stiffened.

The day had darkened. He looked up swiftly at the sun.

It was as if a heavy orange filter had been drawn across its surface. Rolling, enormous and sullen, it burned with a flaming redness just above the western horizon, so dimmed that he could stare directly into it without squinting. Moreover, as he looked down again, unbelieving, he saw the landscape had also changed. It was coated and darkened and shadowed, now, by the all-pervading redness of the sunlight. The color of alizarine red, which was the shade of his own inner, primitive fury, seemed to have escaped from his painting to stain the real landscape now—all earth and sky and water—with the angry color of spilled blood.

2

Miles stood motionless.

A giant's hand seemed to close powerfully about his chest, squeezing the breath out of him. Not breathing, he stared at the changed sun and the red-washed landscape, and an old, old fear dating back to the polio attack—fear of his own traitorous body's finding some way to fail him a second time, before his work could be accomplished—woke inside him.

Grimly he forced himself to breathe and move. He leaned his upper thighs against the heavy shapes of his paint box and cloth-covered painting, pressing them hard against the railing to keep from falling. He rubbed his eyes viciously with the fingers of his good hand and for a painful moment blinked through watery tears at blurred surroundings. But when his gaze cleared again, the redness of sun and land was unchanged, and the fear began to grow into unreasoning anger, like a bubble of fire expanding under his breastbone.

His doctor at the university hospital had told him last month that he was working too hard. His landlady and even Marie Bourtel, who loved him and understood him better than anyone else, had pleaded with him to slow down. So, to be sensible, he had forced himself to get at least six hours' sleep a night these last two weeks—and *still* this false and untrustworthy body had failed him, after all.

With brutal fingers he rubbed his eyes once more. But the color of light and sun would not change. Furiously, helplessly, he looked around the walkway for a phone booth.

Probably, he thought, he should stop using his eyes immediately, so that they would not get any worse. He would phone his doctor. . . .

But the walkway bookstore, holding the only phone in the long passageway, was locked up behind glass doors because it was Sunday. Maybe he could get somebody to help him. . . .

Because it was Sunday, the walkway was all but

deserted. But looking now, Miles saw three other figures near its far end. The nearest of them was a tall, thin, black-haired girl hugging an armful of books to her nearly breastless front. Beyond the girl were a squarely built, blue-suited older man who looked like one of the academic staff and a stocky, sweatered young man with the brown leather scabbard of a slide rule hanging at his belt. Miles started toward them, lugging his paints and canvas.

But then, suddenly, hope leaped faintly within him. For the other three were also staring around themselves with a dazed air. As he watched, they moved toward each other, like people under a huddling instinct in a time of danger. By the time he reached them they were close together and already talking.

"But it has to be something!" the girl was saying shakily, hugging her books to her as if they were a life belt and she afloat on a storm-tossed sea.

"I tell you, it's the end!" said the older man. He was stiff and gray in the face, and he spoke with barely moving, gray lips, holding himself unnaturally erect. The reddened sunlight painted rough highlights on his bloodless face. "The end of the world. The sun's dying. . . ."

"Dying? Are you crazy?" shouted the sweatered young man with the slide rule. "It's dust in the atmosphere. A dust storm south and west of us maybe. Didn't you ever see a sunset—"

"If it's dust, why aren't things darker?" asked the girl. "Everything's clear as before, even the shadows. Only it's red, all red—"

"Dust! Dust, I tell you!" shouted the young man. "It's going to clear up any minute. Wait and see. . . ."

Miles said nothing. But the first leap of hope was expanding into a sense of relief that left him weak at the knees. It was not him then. The suddenly bloody color of the world was not just a subjective illusion caused by his own failing eyesight or exhausted mind, but the result of some natural accident of atmosphere or weather. With the sense of relief, his now-habitual distaste for wasting precious time in social talk woke in him once more. Quietly he turned away and left the other three still talking.

"I tell you," he heard the sweatered young man insisting as he moved off, "it'll have to clear up in a minute. It can't last. . . ."

But it did not clear up, as Miles continued on across the east campus toward his rooming house in the city beyond. On the way he passed other little knots of people glancing from time to time up at the red sun and talking tensely together. Now that his own first reaction to the sun change was over, he found a weary annoyance growing in him at the way they all were reacting.

To a painter, a change in the color values of the daylight could be important. But what was it to them, these muttering, staring people? In any case, as the sweatered young man had said, it would be clearing up shortly.

Pushing the whole business out of his mind, Miles slogged on homeward, feeling the tiredness creeping up in him as the working excitement drained out of him, and his one good arm, for all its unusual development of muscle, began to weary with the labor of lugging canvas and paint box the half mile to his rooming house.

But the subject of the sun change was waiting for him even there. As he walked in the front door of his rooming house at last, he heard his landlady's television set sounding loudly from the living room of her ground-floor apartment.

"No explanation yet from our local weather bureau or the U.S. Meteorological Service. . . ." Miles heard, as he passed the open living-room door. Through it, he had a glimpse of Mrs. Arndahl, the landlady, sitting there with several of the other roomers, silently listening, "No unusual disturbances in the sun or in our own atmosphere have been identified so far, and the expert opinion believes such disturbances could not have taken place without. . . ."

There was a stiffness, an aura of alarm about those watching and listening to the set, that woke annoyance again in Miles. Everyone around him, it seemed, was determined to get worked up about this purely natural event. He stepped by quickly but quietly on the brown carpet before the open door and mounted the equally worn carpet of the stairs to the silence and peace of his own large second-floor room.

There he gratefully laid down at last his canvas and painting tools in their proper places. Then he flopped heavily, still dressed, back down on his narrow bed. The white glass curtain fluttered in the breeze from his half-open window. Weariness flooded through him.

It was a satisfying weariness, in spite of the failure of the afternoon's work—a deep exhaustion, not merely of body and mind, but of imagination and will as well, reflecting the effort he had put into the painting. But still . . . frustration stirred in him once more—that effort had still been nothing more than what was possible to any normal man. It had not been the creative explosion for which he searched.

For the possibility of that explosion was part of his own grim theory of art, the theory he had built up and lived with ever since that day when he had been painting at the foot of the west bluff, four years ago. According to the theory, there should be possible to an artist something much more than any painter had ever achieved up to now. Painting that would be the result of the heretofore normal creative outburst many times multiplied—into an overpassion.

To himself, more prosaically, he called this overpassion "going into overdrive," and it should be no more impossible than the reliably recorded displays of purely physical ability shown by humans under extreme emotional stress—in that phenomenon known as hysterical strength.

Hysterical strength, Miles knew, existed. Not merely because he had evidence of it, but also in the thick manila envelope of newspaper clippings he had collected over the last four years. Clippings like the one about the distraught mother who had lifted the thousands of pounds of her overturned car in order to pull her trapped baby from underneath the vehicle. Or the instance of the bedridden old man in his eighties who had literally run to safety, as cleverly as any slack-wire performer, across a hundred feet of telephone wire to a telephone pole to escape from the third floor of a burning apartment building.

He did not need these things to believe in hysterical strength, because he had experienced it. Himself.

And what the body could do, he told himself again now, wrapped in exhaustion on his bed, the creative spirit

11

should be able to do as well. Someday yet he would tap it artistically—that creative overdrive. And when he did, he would at last tear himself free of that bitterness in him that saw old animal guilts and angers, all the primitive limitations of man—mirrored in everything he tried to reproduce on canvas.

When that moment came, he thought, dully and pleasantly now, sinking into drowsiness, a scene like the one he had painted today would show the future, the promise of Man—instead of a human past of bloody instinct and Stone Age violence underlying all that civilization had built.

The exhaustion lapping around him sucked him slowly down into sleep, like a foundering boat. He let himself sink, unresisting. It was an hour before he was due to meet Marie Bourtel off campus for dinner. Time enough for him to rest a few minutes before washing and dressing to go out. He lay, his thoughts flickering gradually into extinction. . . .

Sleep took him.

When he woke, Miles could not at first remember what time of day it was or why he had wakened. And then it came again—a pounding on his door and the voice of his landlady was calling through it to him.

"Miles! *Miles!*" Mrs. Arndahl's voice came thinly past the door, as if she were pushing it through the crack underneath the door. "Phone call for you! Miles, do you hear me?"

"It's all right. I'm awake," he called back. "I'll be there in a minute."

Groggily he swung his legs over the edge of the bed and sat upright. The single window of his room was a square of night blackness, with the shade not drawn above it. His eyes went to the large round face of the windup alarm clock that stood before the mirror on his dresser. The hands stood at five minutes to ten. He had been asleep at least four hours.

In the mirror his sleep-tousled dark hair, fallen down over his forehead, gave him a wild and savage look. He shoved the hair back and forced himself to his feet. He stumbled across the room, stepped out of the door, and walked numbly down the hall to the upstairs extension phone, which was lying out of its cradle. He picked it up.

"Miles!" It was the soft voice of Marie Bourtel. "Have you been there all this time?"

"Yes," he muttered, still too numb from sleep to wonder why she asked.

"I called a couple of times for you earlier, but Mrs. Arndahl said you hadn't come in yet. I finally had her check your room anyway." The usually calm, gentle voice he was used to hearing on the phone had an unusual edge to it. An edge of something like fear. "Didn't you remember you were going to meet me for dinner at the Lounge?"

"Lounge?" he echoed stupidly. He scrubbed his face with the back of his hand that held the phone, as if to rub memory back into his head. Then contrition flooded him. He remembered the plan to have dinner with Marie at six thirty at the Lounge, which was an off-campus restaurant on the east bank of the river. "Sorry, Marie—I guess I did it again. I was painting this afternoon, and I came back and lay down. I must've fallen asleep."

"Then you're all right." There was relief in Marie's voice for a second; then tension returned. "You don't know what's been happening?"

"Happening?"

"The sun's changed color! About five o'clock this afternoon—"

"Oh, that?" Miles rubbed the back of his hand again over his sleep-numbed face. "Yes, I saw it change. I'd just finished painting—what about it?"

"What about it?" Marie's voice held a sort of wonder. "Miles, *the sun's changed color!*"

"I know," said Miles a little impatiently. But then, rousing him from that first impatience to sudden near anger, came recognition of the relief in Marie's voice a few seconds before, when she had said: "*Then you're all right.*"

Those remembered words jarred unpleasantly back to mind his own first few moments of alarm when he had seen the sun's changed color. He heard the edge in his own voice as he answered her.

"I know the sun's changed color! I said I saw it happen! What of it?"

"Miles—" Marie's voice broke off, oddly, as if she were

13

uncertain of what to say to him. "Miles, I want to see you. If you've been asleep all this time you haven't had dinner yet, have you?"

"Well . . . no. I haven't." Miles was abruptly reminded of the emptiness inside him. Come to think of it, he had not eaten since breakfast, thirteen hours before.

"I'll meet you at the Lounge in ten minutes then," said Marie swiftly. "You can have some dinner, and we can talk. Ten minutes?"

"All right," he said, still somewhat numb with sleep.

"Good-bye, Miles."

"Goodbye."

He hung up.

Slowly waking up in the process, Miles went back to his room, washed his face, put on a fresh shirt and a sport coat, and left the rooming house for the half-mile walk back across the two campuses and their connecting walkway to the business section beyond the east campus. As he passed the landlady's living room, the door was still ajar, and from within he heard the voice of a television announcer, still talking about the change, and saw the backs of a number of people sitting and listening.

The irritation which Marie's concern for him had awakened in him expanded again to include these people. It was ridiculous, almost superstitious of them, to be stampeded into fear just because of what seemed to be a change—undoubtedly temporary, undoubtedly freakish —in the color of the sun.

"*Latest reports over Honolulu say that the redness persists*—" The TV announcer's voice was cut off sharply as Miles softly closed the front door of the house behind him. He headed up the darkened street under the towering, dark-leaved branches of the elms toward the footbridge and the east bank of the river where the Lounge was.

His walk across the campus and over the footbridge was like a walk though an evacuated city. There seemed to be nobody about. But once on the far side of the river, when he pushed open the door of the Lounge, he found the place crowded; only the crowd was all clustered at one end, around the television set at the front of the bar. Forty or fifty people, many of them students, were seated and standing there, packed closely together, listening in ab-

14

solute silence to the same sort of news broadcast he had overheard as he was leaving his rooming house. He threaded his way through them and went back into the rear area where the high-backed wooden booths were; all of these were empty.

Miles took a corner booth in the back of the room. It was the booth he and Marie always took if it was available, and after a few moments their usual waitress, a girl named Joan, a part-time student in the English Department, came through the swinging doors from the kitchen, saw him, and came over to ask him what he wanted.

"Just coffee—two coffees, for now—" Miles remembered suddenly that Marie had said she had already eaten. "I guess just one dinner, come to think of it. Are there any hot beef sandwiches left?"

"Lots of them," said Joan. "Hardly anyone's been eating. They're all listening to television. We're listening, back in the kitchen. —You know the weather people can't figure it out? The sun's actually changed. I mean, it isn't just something in our atmosphere—" She broke off in the face of Miles' silence. "I'll get your coffee."

She went off. She had scarcely brought two cups of coffee back and left again in search of Miles' sandwich when the sound of footsteps from the front of the Lounge made him look up. He saw Marie coming quickly down the aisle between the booths toward him.

She looked at him with the brown eyes that were now so dark and luminous they seemed to have doubled their size in her white face.

"Miles. . . ." She reached across the table to lay her hand on his arm. "Do you feel all right?"

"All right? Me?" He smiled at her, for clearly she needed reassurance. "I'm still a little dopey from sleep and I could stand some food. Outside of that, I'm fine. What's the matter with you?"

She looked at him strangely.

"Miles, you can't be that much out of touch with the rest of the world," she said. "You just *can't*!"

"Oh—" The word came out more harshly than he had meant it to. "You mean this business about the sun changing color? Don't worry, it hasn't done any damage yet.

15

And if it did, that's not my line of work. So why worry about it?"

The waitress came up with Miles' order and said hello to Marie.

"Isn't it terrible? It's still going on," she said to Marie. "'We're all following the news, back in the kitchen. They're just beginning to see it from planes in the South Pacfic now—and it's still red."

She went back to the kitchen.

"I'll tell you why you ought to worry," said Marie quietly and tensely, taking her hand from his arm and sitting back almost huddled in her corner of the booth. "Because it's something that affects the whole world, all the people in the world, and you're one of them."

Automatically he had picked up his fork and begun to eat. Now, at these words, he laid his fork down again. The wave of exhaustion inside him, the wave of anger first pricked to life by the alarm and concern of the people on campus he had passed on his way back to the rooming house, returned with force to wash his appetite away. The mashed potatoes and gravy he had just put into his mouth seemed to have no more taste than if they were made of flour and water and artificial coloring.

"The other two billion won't miss me if I stick to my own work," he said. "I've got more important things to worry about. I spent all day today painting the river bluffs and the freeway bridge. Do you want to know how it came out?"

"I can guess how it came out," answered Marie. She too was a student in the school of art at the university. Like Miles, she was graduating this spring. Unlike Miles, she had neither a grant for European study waiting for her nor the supporting belief of her instructors that she had the makings of a truly unusual artist in her. It did not help that Miles himself could see promise in her work. For even he could not bring himself to class that promise with what he himself was after in painting.

"Marie," an instructor had said bluntly to Miles one day in a burst of frankness, "is going to be good—possibly quite good—if she works hard at it. You're either going to be unmatchable or impossible."

Yet in spite of this, there were elements in Marie's work

16

which were the equivalent of those very elements for which Miles searched in his own. Where he was stark, she was beautiful; where he was violent, she was gentle. Only, he wanted his equivalents of these things on a different level from that on which she had found hers.

"Well, it was the same thing all over again," said Miles. He picked up the fork once more and mechanically tried to force himself to eat. "The painting turned savage on me—as usual."

"Yes," answered Marie in a low voice, "and I know why."

He looked up sharply from his plate at her and found her eyes more brilliant upon him than ever.

"And this business about the sun proves it," she went on, more strongly. "I don't mean the change in color itself; I mean the way you're reacting to it—" She hesitated, then burst out with a rush. "I've never said this to you, Miles. But I always knew I'd have to say it someday, and now this thing's happened and the time's come! You aren't *ever* going to find the answer to what's bothering you about the way you paint. You never will because you won't look in the right direction. You'll look everywhere but there!"

"What do you mean?" He stared at her, the cooling hot beef sandwich now completely forgotten. "And what's this business of the sun got to do with it?"

"It's got everything to do with it," she said tightly, taking hold of her edge of the table with both hands, as if her grip on it were a grip on him, forcing him to stand still and listen to her. "Maybe this change in the color of the sun hasn't hurt anything yet—that's true. But it's frightened a world full of people! And *that* doesn't mean anything to you. Don't you understand me, Miles? The trouble with you is you've got to the point where something like this can happen, and a world full of people be frightened to death by it—and you don't react at all!"

He looked narrowly at her.

"You're telling me I'm too wound up in my painting?" he asked. "Is that it?"

"*No!*" Marie answered fiercely. "You're just not interested enough in the rest of life!"

"The rest of life?" he echoed. "Why, of course not! All

17

the rest of life does for me is get between me and the painting—and I need every ounce of energy I can get for work. What's wrong with that?"

"You know what's wrong!" Marie started out of her corner and leaned across the table toward him. "You're too strong, Miles. You've got to the point where nothing frightens you anymore—and that's not natural. You're all one-sided, like that overdeveloped arm of yours and nothing on the other side—" Abruptly she began to cry, but silently, the tears streaming down her face, even while her voice went on, low and tight and controlled as before.

"Oh, I know that's a terrible thing to say!" she said. "I didn't want to say it to you, Miles. I didn't! But it's true. You're all one huge muscle in the part of you that's a painter, and there's nothing left in you on the human side at all. And *still* you're not satisfied. You keep on trying to make yourself even more one-sided, so that you can be a bloodless, camera-eyed observer! Only, it can't be done—and it *shouldn't* be done! You can't go on in this way without destroying yourself. You'll turn yourself into a painting machine and still never get what you want, because it really isn't pictures on canvas you're after, Miles. It's people! It really is! Miles—"

Her words broke off and echoed away into the silence of the empty dining area at the back of the Lounge. Into that silence, from the bar at the front, came the unintelligible murmur of the announcer speaking from the television set and still relaying news, or the lack of it, about the sudden change of color of the sun. Miles sat without moving, staring at her. Finally, he found the words for which he was reaching.

"Is this what you called me up, and asked me to meet you here, to say?" he asked, at last.

"Yes!" answered Marie.

He still sat, staring at her. There was a hard, heavy feeling of loneliness and pain just above his breastbone. He had thought that at least there was one person in the universe who understood what he was trying to do. One person, anyway, who had some vision of that long road and that misty goal toward which he was reaching with every ounce of strength he had and every waking hour of his days. He had thought that Marie understood. Now it was plain she did not. She was, in the end, as blind as the rest of them.

If only she had understood, she would have realized that it was people he had been striving to get free of, right from the start. He had been trying to pull himself out of the quicksand of their bloody history and narrow lives, so that he would be able to see clearly, hear clearly, and work without their weight clinging to his mind and hampering the freedom of his mind's eye.

But Marie had evidently never seen this fact, any more than the rest.

He got to his feet, picked up his check and hers, and walked away from her to the cashier and out of the Lounge without another word.

Outside, still the streets were all but deserted. And through this desert cityscape, under a full moon made dusky by the reflection of reddened sunlight, he returned slowly to his rooming house.

3

In the night he woke suddenly for no apparent reason. He lay staring at the darkness of the ceiling above him and wondering what had wakened him at such an hour. The bedroom was hot and stuffy, and he had kicked off all his covers.

His pajama top was wet with perspiration. It clung like a clammy hand to his chest, and this, plus the thickness of the air, filled him with a strange sense of some lurking presence as of a crouching danger in the dark. He wondered whether Marie was sleeping peacefully or whether she had also wakened.

It was unnatural for the room to to be so stuffy and hot. He got up and went to open the window, but it already stood wide open from the bottom, as high as it could be raised. Outside, the night air hung unmoving, as unnaturally warm and stuffy as the room air.

No breeze stirred. Below, silhouetted against the corner streetlight beyond, a tall, horizontal-armed oak towered over the lilac bushes and the small flowering crab tree in the dark rooming house yard. Bushes and trees alike stood like forms of poured concrete, all stiffly upright, darker than the night.

Distantly, thunder muttered. Miles looked up and out at the horizon above the trees, and the flicker of heat lightning jumped, racing across the arc of black sky in which no moon or stars were showing. The thunder came again, more loudly.

He stood watching as the lightning and thunder increased. Still no breath of air moved. The lightning flared along the distant edge of darkness like the cannon flashes of some titanic war of the gods, just out of sight over the horizon. The thunder grew. Now the heat lightning had given way to chain lightning, which stitched wild, jagged thrusts of brilliance across the sky.

The air sighed suddenly outside the window. It blew damply against him. The thunder roared. Suddenly the skies split with thunder directly above him, and a lightning flash left a searing afterimage of trees and bushes painted on his vision. The wind blasted, and suddenly there was a dry, hard pattering all around.

It was hail. At once, before he could move back and close the window, the full hailstorm was on him. In the wild lightning he saw the yard below full of dancing whiteness, saw the bushes bent over and even the ornamental flowering crab tree bent nearly to the earth.

Only the oak, he noticed, refused to bend. It stood towering as before. Its leaves lay over flat, and its branches swayed to the wind, but its trunk ignored the storm. It stood unyielding, upright, all but indifferent.

Hail was stinging Miles' face and arms. He pulled back from the window, closing it all but an inch or two. Even through that little space, the wind whistled icily into the room. He got back into bed, huddling the covers up around him.

Before he knew it, he was asleep once more.

"The Ship. . . ."

It seemed that those were almost the first words Miles encountered on going downstairs after waking the next morning. They were on the lips of his landlady as he left for breakfast and his first class, and they echoed around him from everybody who was abroad in the red light of this early day as he crossed the campus. When he reached the room in which the seminar on Renaissance art was held, it seemed to be the only topic of conversation among the graduate students there as well.

"Too big to land, anyway," Mike Jarosh, a short, bearded man who was one of the graduate history majors, was saying as Miles came in. "As big as the state of Rhode Island."

"They'll probably send down a smaller ship," somebody else put in.

"Maybe. Maybe not," Mike said. "Remember, the ship just appeared there, in orbit a thousand miles out. None of the telescopes watching the sun saw it coming, and it appeared right in front of the sun, right in front of their telescopes. If whoever's in the ship can do that, they may be able to send down people to the surface of the Earth here just by some way of transferring them suddenly from the ship to here—"

The professor in charge of the seminar, Wallace Hankins, a thin, stooped man, half-bald but with his remaining hair still as black as his eyebrows, came in the door just then, cutting off Mike in mid-sentence.

"Any news? Any broadcasts from the ship—" Mike was beginning to ask him, when Hankins cut him short.

"Yes, there's been some kind of message," Hankins said. "The United Nations Secretary-General just received it—the broadcasts don't say how or why. But that's all beside the point. It's plain there's no use trying to hold any kind of seminar under these conditions. So we won't try it today. The rest of you go about your business—and, with luck, we'll meet again here next week at the same time under conditions more conducive to a discussion of Renaissance art."

The babble of excitement that broke out at this announcement, Miles thought, would have suited a group of grade-school children better than a dozen hardworking graduate students. The others hurried off as, more slowly, he put his own books back into the briefcase from which he had taken them while Mike Jarosh was talking. Hankins had stood aside to let the class members stampede past him out the open door. So it happened that, as Miles was leaving last, he came face to face with Hankins.

"I'm sorry to lose a day," said Miles honestly, stopping.

Hankins looked back at him, his round face under the high, hairless forehead more than a little sour.

"The Renaissance seems out of fashion at the moment," he said and, following Miles out through the door of the seminar room, closed it behind both of them.

Miles, briefcase in hand, headed back down the worn marble steps of the staircase inside the history building and out of the building back toward his rooming house. He was not quite sure what he should do with this unexpected gap in his daily schedule. Automatically, he thought of setting up his easel somewhere outside and trying to work—and then he remembered that outdoor painting would be all but impossible as long as the sun continued to be this color. Color values would be all off.

No sooner had he thought of this than he was intrigued by the notion of doing a painting under the red light, just so that he could see in what way the colors were off once the sun returned to normal. He hurried on to the rooming house and went up the stairs to his room with enthusiasm beginning to burn inside him. But as he entered his room, his spirits took a sudden drop. The sight of the canvas he had painted yesterday afternoon, now drying in the corner, reminded him abruptly of Marie and the storm of the night before.

He was sudddenly face to face with a strong sense of guilt and loss. No matter how wrong Marie had been last evening, two things remained unchanged. It was her concern for him that had made her say what she had and also, he had no one else in the world that was close to him.

He sat down heavily on the edge of his bed, newly made by Mrs. Arndahl. The strap springs creaked dolefully under his weight. He had been looking forward to the release and freedom of his year in Europe. The thought of loneliness had never occurred to him until now. But now he felt it come to him powerfully at the thought that he might easily lose Marie for good.

He got abruptly to his feet. He had been wrong in walking out like that. It had not been fair to expect her to understand what moved him in his wholehearted search without ever a word of explanation of that search. At least he could find her and make that explanation now. He owed her that much.

He got up, went over to open the top drawer of his dresser to take out a brown manila envelope. He put it into the inside pocket of his jacket and headed back out of the rooming house.

At this hour Marie was usually in the second-floor study room of the university library. But when he got there, he found the room deserted except for three or four stray figures looking dwarfed and foolish among the long tables and empty chairs. Marie was not one of them. He turned and left the library.

The most logical place to look next was the girls' dormitory, in which Marie was a counselor.

He went there. It was on the other side of the campus, a tall red-brick building with a row of glass doors across the front of it. He went through one of the doors into the lobby and asked for Marie at the desk. The clerk buzzed Marie's room, and less than a minute later Marie herself called down on the house phone. Miles heard her voice with a sense of relief.

"It's me," he said. "Can you come down?"

"I'll be right there," her voice answered. His heart moved in him. It was the same soft, calm voice as ever. He had expected any reaction but this, after he had walked out on her the way he had the night before.

"You can wait in the lounge," the pointed-faced little clerk said to him.

He had waited in that lounge many times before, but when he went in now, like everything else, it was different. Usually there were only four or five vaguely impatient or irritated males seated in the heavy armchairs and couches scattered decorously about the room. Now nearly all the farther seats were empty. The nearer ones had been drawn in around the television set and were occupied by a small crowd of girls. These listened to the omnipresent television announcer in such uniform silence that Miles had no difficulty overhearing what the announcer was saying.

"Word has been received from reliable sources here at the UN," the announcer was saying, "that the message was not sent by any mechanical means from the ship now

23

in orbit about our world but was delivered in person by two of the passengers or crew from the ship. The same source also provides the information that the two beings in question appear to be two men with somewhat swarthy features, in every respect, including the suits they wear, as human as we are. Further word is expected shortly.

"Now some details about the ship, as the details have been gleaned by telescope from the surface of our world. The ship itself appears to be at least as large as was originally estimated. There seems to be no evidence of windows or entrances in its outer surface. Moreover, no sign has been seen of a small ship leaving it or of any means by which the two from the ship could have made the trip down to the UN buildings here in New York. No landing of any type of alien craft has been reported and no unusual visitors have been escorted to the building. . . ."

His voice droned on. Miles went to the opposite end of the room and sat down on a heavy green sofa pushed back against the wall. It was only a few minutes before Marie appeared in the entrance to the lounge. He got up swiftly and went to meet her.

"Miles—" she said as he came up to her.

"Can we get out of here?" he said. "Somewhere away from television sets and radios?"

"I'm on duty here at the dorm starting at one o'clock," she answered. "But we could go someplace and have an early lunch until then."

"Good," he said. "Let's go to someplace downtown that isn't overrun by people from the U."

They took the bus toward downtown Minneapolis. As the bus rolled across the freeway bridge, Miles gestured toward the window beside which Marie was sitting.

"Look," he said, indicating the rock wall below which he had stood painting the afternoon before. "You see the bluff there? Do you think you could climb it?"

Marie stared at the steep rise of rock.

"I guess so—if I had to," she said. She turned, frowning in puzzlement at him. "I don't think I'd like to. Why?"

"I'll tell you later, while we're having lunch," said Miles. "But look at it now—will you?—and just imagine yourself climbing it."

Marie looked back out of the window and kept her eyes on the bluff until the bus passed the point where that side of the river could be seen. Then she looked questioningly at Miles.

When he said nothing, however, she looked away, and neither of them said anything more until they left the bus downtown.

Miles, in fact, waited until they were actually inside the restaurant they had picked—a small, medium-priced eating place with no television set.

"About last night—" he began, after the waitress had given them menus and left.

Marie laid down her menu. She reached out across the table to put her hand on his.

"Never mind," she said. "It doesn't matter."

"But it does matter," he answered. He withdrew his hand, took the manila envelope out from the inside pocket of his jacket, and handed it to her. "There's something I want you to understand. That's why I had you look at that bluff on the way here. I should have told you about it a long time ago; but when I first met you, well, I just wasn't used to telling anyone about it, and later I liked to think you understood without being told. Then, when I found you didn't last night—that's why I blew up. Take a look in that envelope."

Looking strangely at him, Marie opened the envelope and poured out the sheaf of yellowing newspaper clippings on the white place mat. She looked through them while he waited. Then she looked back up at him, frowning.

"I guess I *don't* understand," she said.

"They're all instances of hysterical strength," Miles said. "Have you ever heard of that?"

"I think so," she said, still frowning. "But what's it all got to do with you?"

"It ties in with what I believe," he said. "A theory of mine about painting. About anything creative, actually . . ." And he told her about it. But when he was done, she still shook her head.

"I didn't know," she said. She shuffled the clippings with her fingers. "But, Miles, isn't it a pretty big guess on your part? These"—she shuffled the clippings, again looking down at them——"are hard enough to believe——"

"Will you believe me if *I* tell you something?" he interrupted.

"Of course!" Her head came up.

"All right then. Listen," he said, "before I met you, when I first had polio, I took up painting mainly to give myself an excuse to hide from people." He took a deep breath. "I couldn't get over the fact I was crippled, you see. I had a knack for art, but the painting and drawing were just an excuse that first year, after I'd been sick."

"Miles," she said gently, reaching out to put her hand on his again.

"But then, one day, something happened," he said. "I was outside painting——at the foot of the bluff I pointed out to you. And something clicked. Suddenly I was in it——*inside* the painting. I can't describe it. And I forgot everything around me."

He stopped and drew a deep breath.

"I shouldn't have done that," he said. "Because it just happened I was attracting a gallery. Some kids had come up to watch me painting. Kids not much younger than I was——and I guess after a while they must have started asking me questions. But I didn't even hear them. I was all wrapped up in what I was painting, for the first time——and it was like a miracle, like coming alive for the first time since I'd been sick."

In spite of himself, remembering, his hand curled into a fist under her fingers. She held tightly to the fist.

"When I didn't answer," he went on after a second, "they evidently began to think that I was embarrassed by being caught painting, and they began to jostle me and move my brushes. But I was still just barely conscious of them, and I was scared stiff at the thought of quitting work on that painting, even for a second. I had a feeling that if I quit, even for that long, I'd lose it——this *in*-ness I'd discovered. But finally, one of them grabbed up my paint box and ran off with it, and I had to come out of it."

"Oh, Miles!" said Marie, softly. Her fingertips soothed his hard-clenched fist.

"So I chased him——the one who'd taken it. And when I was just about to grab him, he dropped it. So I brought it back—and then I found out something. My canvas was gone."

"They took it?" said Marie. "Miles, they didn't!"

"I looked around," he went on, seeing not her across the table as much as the much-remembered scene in his mind's eye, "and finally, I spotted the one who'd taken it. He'd run off the other way from the one who took my paints and up around the road leading to the top of the bluff, and now he was running along the bluff overhead."

Miles stopped speaking. With an effort he pulled his inner gaze from the four-year-old memory and looked again at Marie.

"Marie," he said, "I wasn't thinking of anything but that painting. It seemed like life itself to me, just then, life I'd found again after thinking I'd lost it for good with polio. It seemed to me that I had to have that painting, no matter what happened. And I went and got it."

He hesitated.

"Marie," he said, "I climbed up that bluff and got in front of the kid who'd taken it. When he saw me coming, he threw it facedown on the grass and ran. When I picked it up, it was nothing but smears and streaks of paint with grass sticking all over it."

"Miles!" said Marie, her fingers tightening on his fist. "How terrible!"

"No," said Miles, "not terrible." He looked deeply into her brown eyes. "Wonderful. Marie, don't you understand! *I climbed up that cliff!*"

She stared back at him, baffled.

"I know, you said that," she said. "And you must have climbed awfully fast—"

"Yes, but that's not it!" said Miles. "Listen! I climbed up that cliff—and I had only one arm. Only one arm and one hand to climb with!"

She still stared, without understanding.

"Of course," she said. "That's right, you only had one arm—" She broke off suddenly, on a quick intake of breath.

"Yes. You see?" Miles heard his own voice, sounding almost triumphant. "Marie, a cliff like that can't be climbed by a one-handed man. You need to hold with one hand while you move the other to a fresh handhold, and so on. I came back there the next day and tried to see if I could climb it again. And I couldn't. I couldn't even get started. The only way I could possibly have done it would have been to balance on my feet alone while I changed handholds."

He nodded at the clippings on the place mat before her.

"To climb like that," he said, "I'd have needed the strength and speed written about in those news clippings."

She gazed at him, her face a little pale.

"You don't remember how you did it?" she asked at last.

He shook his head.

"It's all sort of a blur," he said. "I remember wanting to go up the cliff, and I remember climbing up it, somehow, very quickly and easily, and the next thing I knew, I was facing the kid with my painting." He stopped, but she said nothing. "You see why I lost my head with you last night? I thought you understood that what I was after was something that didn't leave any strength or time left over for the rest of the world. I thought you understood it without being told. It wasn't until after that I began to see how unfair I was being in expecting you to understand something like this without knowing what I'd been through and what I was after."

He pulled his hand out from under her now-quiet fingers and took her hand instead in his own grasp.

"But you understand now, don't you?" he asked. "You do, don't you?"

To his surprise she shivered suddenly, and her face grew even more pale.

"Marie!" he said. "Don't you understand—"

"Oh, I do. I understand. Of course, Miles." Her hand turned so that her fingers grasped his. "It's not that. It's just that knowing this now somehow makes it all that much worse."

"Worse?" He stared at her.

"I mean"—her voice trembled—"all this business about the sun and the ship and the two men, or whatever they are. I've had a feeling from the beginning that it all meant something terrible for us—for you and me. And now, somehow, your telling me this makes me even more afraid."

"What of?" he asked.

"I don't know." He could feel her shiver again, just barely feel it, but the shiver was there. "Something . . . something that's going to come between us—"

From across the room a sudden, measured voice interrupted her. Looking in that direction, Miles saw that two men had just entered the restaurant and sat down at a table against the farther wall. On the table one of them placed a portable radio, and even with the volume turned down, its voice carried across to the table where he sat with Marie. Anger exploded in him.

"I'll make them turn that thing down!" he said, starting to get to his feet. But Marie caught hold of his arm.

"No," she said. "Sit down. Please, sit down, Miles. Listen—"

"By television and radio," the radio was saying. "We now bring you the President of the United States, speaking to you directly from the East Room of the White House. . . ." The musical strains of "Hail to the Chief" followed closely upon the announcer's words. Marie got quickly to her feet.

"Miles, quickly," she said. "Let's find a television set."

"Marie—" he began harshly, with the backwash of his anger at the two men and the radio across the room in his voice. Then he saw the peculiar rigidity of her face, and a feeling of uneasiness washed in to drown the fury.

"All right," he said, getting to his feet in turn, "if you want to."

She hurried out of the restaurant, and he had to stretch his legs to keep up with her. Outside, in the sudden glare of red sunlight, she paused and looked, almost frantically, right and left.

"Where?" she asked. "Oh, where, Miles?"

"The nearest bar, I suppose," he said. Looking about himself, he spotted the neon sign of one, palely lit and violet-colored in the red sunlight, half a block down the street from them. "This way."

They went quickly down the half block and into the bar. Within, no one was moving—neither bartenders nor customers. They all were sitting or standing still as carvings, staring at the large television set set up high on a dark wooden shelf at the inner end of the bar. From that ledge, the lined, rectangular face of the President of the United States looked out. Miles heard the tail end of his sentence as they entered.

"For simultaneous announcement to all countries of the world," said the slow, pausing voice in the same heavy tones they had heard a dozen times before, speaking on smaller issues of the country and the world. "These two visitors also supplied us with a film strip to be used in conjunction with the announcement. First, here is a picture of our two friends from the civilization of worlds at the center of our galaxy."

The rectangular face disappeared, to be replaced by the still image of two men in what seemed to be gray business suits, standing before a window in some sort of lounge or reception room—probably a room in one of the UN buildings, Miles thought.

It was as the radio announcer had said earlier. There was nothing about the two to distinguish them from any other humans. Their noses were a little long, the skin of their faces a little dark, and there was a suspicion of a mongoloid fold above the eyes. Otherwise, they might have been encountered on the streets of any large city in the world, east or west, without the slightest suspicion that they had come from anywhere off the planet.

"These gentlemen," the Presidential voice went on slowly, "have explained to the representatives of the nations of our world that our galaxy, that galaxy of millions upon millions of stars, of which our sun is a minor star out near the edge"—the figures of the two men disappeared and were replaced by what looked like a glowing spiral of dust floating against a black background—"will shortly be facing attack by a roving intergalactic race which periodically preys upon those island universes like our galaxy which dot that intergalactic space.

"Their civilization, which represents many worlds in many solar systems in toward the center of the galaxy, has taken the lead in forming a defensive military force which will attempt to meet these predators at the edge of our galaxy and turn them aside from their purpose. They inform us that if the predators are not turned aside, over ninety percent of the life on the inhabited worlds of our galaxy will be captured and literally processed for food to feed this nomadic and rapacious civilization. Indeed, it is the constant need to search for sustenance for their overwhelming numbers that keeps them always on the move between and through the galaxies, generation succeeding generation in rapacious conquest."

Suddenly the image of something like a white-furred weasel, with hands on its two upper limbs and standing erect on its two hind limbs, filled the television screen. Beside it was the gray outline of a man, and it could be seen that the creature came about shoulder-high on the outline.

"This," said the disembodied voice of the Chief Executive, "is a picture of what the predator looks like, according to our two visitors. The predator is born, lives, and dies within his ship or ships in space. His only concern is to survive—first as a race, then as an individual. His numbers are countless. Even the ships in which he lives will probably be numbered in the millions. He and his fellows will be prepared to sustain staggering losses if they can win their way into the feeding ground that is our galaxy. Here, by courtesy of our two visitors, is a picture of what the predator fleet will look like. Collectively, they're referred to in the records of our galaxy as the Silver Horde."

Once more the image in the television screen changed.

"This is one of their ships," said the President's voice.

A spindle-shaped craft of some highly polished metal appeared on the television screen. Beside it, the silhouette of a man had shrunk until it was approximately the size of a human being standing next to a double trailer truck.

"This is a scout ship, the smallest of their craft—holding a single family, usually consisting of three or four adults and perhaps as many young."

The image on the televistion set shrank almost to a dot, and beside it appeared a large circular craft nearly filling the screen.

"And this is the largest of their ships," said the President. "Inside, it should have much the appearance and population of a small city—up to several thousand individuals, adult and young, and at least one large manufacturing or tool-making unit required by the Horde for maintenance and warfare, as well as food-processing and storage units."

The voice of the Chief Executive lifted, on a note that signaled he was approaching the end of what he had to say.

"Our visitors have told us," he said, "that defense of the galaxy is a common duty. For our world to join in that defense is therefore a duty. What they require from us, however, is a contribution of a highly specialized nature." His voice hesitated and then went on more strongly. "They tell us that the weapons with which our galaxy's defensive force will meet the Horde are beyond the understanding of our science here on Earth. They tell us, however, that they are part physical, part nonphysical in nature. The number of fighting individuals we can contribute, therefore, to our galaxy's defense is limited by our relatively primitive state of awareness as far as these nonphysical forces are concerned. We can send only one man. This one individual—this one man who is best suited to be our representative by natural talent and abilities—has already been selected by our visitors. He will shortly be taken over by them, adjusted so as to make the best possible use of these talents, and then turned loose for a brief period to move about our world and absorb an identification with the rest of us. This process of absorbing an identification has been compared by our visitors to the process of charging a car battery, to exposing its plates to a steady input of electrical current. Once he has been so 'charged,' all of us on this world who have managed to contribute to the 'charging' will continue to have some sort of awareness in the backs of our minds of what he is going through up on the battle line, to which he will then be transported. And from this linkage he will draw the personal nonphysical strength with which he will operate his particular weapon when the enounter with the Horde occurs."

The President's face once more appeared on the television screen. He paused, and standing in the bar, Miles felt the impact of the older man's eyes upon him—as, evidently, did everyone else in the room.

"That is all for now," said the President slowly. "As soon as we have more information, people of America and people of our world, it will be released to you. Meanwhile, in this trying and strange time into which we have suddenly been plunged by events, let me ask you all to go on with your lives in their ordinary fashion and show patience. As we approach what lies in store for us, what lies in store for us will become more plain to us all. God bless you, and good afternoon."

His face vanished from the screen. There was a moment of grayness; then the face of an announcer flickered on.

"The voice you have just heard," the announcer said smoothly, "was that of the President of the United States. . . ."

There was a slowly beginning, gradually increasing combination of sighs and rustles of movement within the bar as the people there came to life and action again. Miles turned to Marie and saw her standing white-faced, still staring at the television screen.

"Come on," said Miles. "Let's get out of here."

He had to take her by the arm before he could break the trance that held her. But when he touched her, she started and seemed to come awake. She turned obediently and followed him out once more into the red-lighted street.

In the street she leaned against him, as if the strength had gone out of her. He put his arm around her to steady her and looked anxiously about him. Two blocks down the street, a lone cab was coming toward them. Miles whistled, and the cab came on, angling into the curb to stop before them.

Miles bent down to open the rear door. As he did, he became conscious of the fact that besides the driver, there was a man in a blue suit in the front seat and another man sittting in the back seat. He checked, with the door half-open.

"It's all right," said the man in the back seat. "You're Miles Vander, aren't you? And this will be Miss Bourtel."

He reached into his inside suitcoat pocket and brought out a leather case, which he flipped open. Miles saw a card in a plastic case, with the man's picture and some lines of fine type underneath.

"Treasury Department," said the man. "You're to come with us, Mr. Vander. We'll drop Miss Bourtel off on the way."

Miles stared at him.

"Please get in," said the man in the front seat beside the driver, and the evenness of his tone made the words more a command than an invitation. "We were told we'd find you here. And there's no time to lose."

Within the circle of Miles' arm, Marie leaned even more heavily against him. Worry for her tightened Miles' chest.

"All right," he said abruptly. He helped Marie into the back seat of the taxi next to the man sitting there and then got in himself, closing the door behind him.

"We'd better go—" he was beginning, when the man in the front seat cut him short.

"That's all right. We've got our instructions on that, too," he said. He sat half turned in the front seat, with one elbow over the back of the seat so that he looked directly into Miles' face. "Look at her."

Alarmed, Miles looked sharply around again at Marie. She sat with her head against him, her eyes closed, unmoving, breathing deeply and slowly.

"Don't worry," said the man in the front seat. "She's only asleep. The aliens arranged it—the two from the ship—to get her through the business of seeing you picked up by us. We're to deliver her to the university hospital, where they'll take care of her for an hour or two, until she wakes. When she does wake up, she won't be alarmed about what's happened to you anymore."

Miles stared at him.

"What *is* all this?" Miles burst out.

"I don't blame you for not suspecting," the man in the front seat answered. The taxi was already pulling away from the curb and heading off down the street in the direction of the distant university. "We'll be taking you immediately to the airport, where a military airplane will fly you to Washington. You're the man that the two aliens from the spaceship—our two visitors from the center of the galaxy—have picked to be this world's representative, defending the galaxy against the Silver Horde, and everything we've done so far, like our finding you and Miss Bourtel's falling asleep, has been arranged by them."

34

4

The process by which Miles was whirled away after that to the university hospital, where they left Marie sleeping, to the airport, by jet to Washington, by blue civilian sedan there to a large building which he dimly recognized as the Pentagon, and within the Pentagon to a suite of rooms more resembling a hotel suite than anything else—all this passed like the successive shapes of some bad dream. And after all the rushing was over, after he had at last been settled in the suite of rooms, he discovered that he had nothing to do but wait.

The two men who had picked him up in Minneapolis and brought him here stayed with him through the dinner hour. After the dinner cart with its load of clinking empty plates and dirty silverware had been wheeled out again, the two men watched television, with its endless parade of announcers, throughout the evening—the sound turned low at Miles' request. Miles himself, after prowling restlessly around the room and asking a number of questions to which his guardians gave noncommittal answers, finally settled down with a pencil and some notepaper to while away his time making sketches of the other two.

He had become lost in this, to the point where he no longer noticed the murmur of the television or the passage of time, when there was a knock at his door and one of the guards got up to answer. A moment later Miles was conscious that the man had returned and was standing over him, waiting for him to look up from his sketching. Miles looked up.

"The President's here," said the guard.

Miles stared, then got hastily to his feet, putting his sketches aside. Beyond the guard, he saw the door to his suite standing open and a moment later heard the approach of feet down the polished surface of the corridor outside. These came closer and closer. A second later the man Miles had been watching on television earlier that day walked into the room.

In person, the Chief Executive was not as tall as he often appeared in pictures—no taller than Miles himself.

Close up, however, he looked more youthful than he appeared in news photos and on television. He shook hands with Miles with a great deal of warmth, but it was something of the warmth of a tired and worried man who can only snatch a few moments from his day in which to be human and personal.

He put a hand on Miles' shoulder and walked him over to a window that looked out on a narrow strip of grass in what appeared to be a small artificial courtyard under some kind of skylight. The two men who had been with Miles and the others who had come with the Chief Executive quietly slipped out the door of the suite and left them alone.

"It's an honor . . ." said the President. He still stood with his hand on Miles' shoulder, and his voice was deep with the throatiness of age. "It's an honor to have an American be the one who was chosen. I wanted to tell you that myself."

"Thank you . . . Mr. President," Miles answered, stumbling a little over the unfamiliar words of the title. He burst out then in spite of the urgings of courtesy. "But I don't know why they'd want to pick me! Why me?"

The older man's hand patted his shoulder a little awkwardly, even a little bewilderedly.

"I don't know either," murmured the President. "None of us knows."

"But—" Miles hesitated, then plunged ahead. "We've only got their word for everything. How do we know it's true, what they say?"

Again the Presidential hand patted him sympathetically on the shoulder.

"We don't know," the older man said, looking out at the grass of the artificial courtyard. "That's the truth of the matter. We don't know. But that ship of theirs is something—incredible. It backs up their story. And after all, they only want—"

He broke off, looked at Miles, and smiled a little apologetically.

Miles felt a sudden coldness inside him.

"You mean," he said slowly, "you're ready to believe them because they want only one man? Because they want only me?"

"That's right," said the Chief Executive. He did not pat Miles on the shoulder now. He looked directly into Miles' eyes. "They've asked for nothing but one man. And they've shown us some evidence—shown us heads of state, that is—some physical evidence from the last time the Horde went through the galaxy millions of years ago. We've seen the dead body of one of the Horde—preserved, of course. We've seen samples of the weapons and tools of the Horde. Of course, these could have been fakes—made up just to show us. But, Miles—" He paused, still keeping Miles' eyes locked with his own. "The best guess we can make is that they're telling the truth."

Miles opened his mouth to speak, then closed it again, helplessly.

Finally, he got the words out.

"But," he said, "if they're lying. . . ."

The President straightened. Once more he put his hand on Miles' shoulder, in a curious touch—a touch like an accolade, as if he were knighting Miles.

"Of course," he said slowly, "if it should turn out to be that . . . your responsibility might turn out to be even greater than it is."

They stood facing each other. Suddenly Miles understood—just as in the same moment he understood that it was just this message that the other man had come personally to give him. It was clear, if unspoken, between them. Yet Miles felt a strange, angry need to bring the understanding out in the open. A need to make it plain the thing was there, like touching with his tongue, again and again, the exposed root of an aching tooth.

"You mean, if it turns out that they want to make me into something dangerous to people back here," he said, "you want me to do something about it, is that it?"

The President did not answer. He continued to look at Miles and hold Miles' shoulder as if he were pledging him to some special duty.

"You mean," said Miles again, more loudly, "that if it turns out that I'm being made into something dangerous to . . . the human race, I'm to destroy myself. Is that it?"

The President sighed, and his hand dropped from Miles'

shoulder. He turned to look out at the grass in the court-yard.

"You're to follow your own judgment," he said to Miles.

A great loneliness descended upon Miles. A chilling loneliness. He had never felt so alone before. It seemed as if the President's words had lifted him up and transported him off, far off, from all humanity into an isolated watchtower, to a solitary sentry post far removed from all the rest of humanity. He too turned and looked out at the little strip of grass. Suddenly it looked greener and more beautiful than any such length of lawn he had ever gazed upon in his life. It seemed infinitely precious.

"Miles," he heard the older man say.

He lifted his head and turned to see the President facing him once more, with his hand outstretched.

"Good luck, Miles," said the President.

"Thank you." Miles took the hand automatically. They shook hands, and the Chief Executive turned and walked away across the room and out the door, leaving it open. The two Treasury agents who had picked up Miles originally came back in, shutting the door firmly behind them. They sat down again without a word near the TV set and turned it on. Miles heard its low murmur again in his ear.

Almost blindly, he himself turned and walked into one of the two bedrooms of the suite, closing the door behind him. He lay down on the bed on his back, staring at the white ceiling.

He woke suddenly—and only by his waking was he made aware of the fact that his drifting thoughts had dwindled into sleep. Standing over him, alongside the bed, were two figures that were vaguely familiar, although he could not remember ever having seen them before in his life. Slowly he remembered. They were the two figures, still business-suited, that had been shown on the television screen as he and Marie had watched the President's broadcast in the bar. Suddenly he understood. These were the two aliens from the monster ship that overhung Earth, under a sun that they had colored red to attract the attention of all the people on the world to the coming of that ship.

Reflex, the reflex that brings an animal out of sound

38

sleep to its feet, brought Miles to his. He found himself standing almost between the two aliens. At close range their faces looked directly into his, no less human of feature or color or general appearance than they had looked before. But this close, it seemed to Miles that he felt an emanation from them—something too still, too composed to be human. And yet the eyes they fixed upon him were not unkind.

Only remote, as remote as the eyes of men on some high plateau looking down into a jungle of beasts.

"Miles," said the one on his left, who was slightly the shorter of the two. His voice was a steady baritone—calm, passionless, distant, without foreign accent. "Are you ready to come with us?"

Still fogged by sleep, still with his nerves wound wiretight by the animal reflex that had jerked him up out of slumber, Miles snapped out what he might not have said without thinking, otherwise.

"Do I have a choice?"

The two looked steadily at him.

"Of course you have a choice," said the shorter of the two calmly. "You'd be no good, to your world or to us, unless you wanted to help us."

Miles began to laugh. It was harsh, reflexive laughter that burst from him almost without intention. It took him a few seconds to get it under control, but finally, he did.

"Want to?" he said—his real feelings bursting out in spite of himself. "Of course I don't want to. Yesterday I had my own life, with its future all planned out. Now the sun turns red, and it seems I have to go to some impossible place and do some impossible thing—instead of what I've been planning and working toward for five years! And you ask me if I *want* to!"

He stared at them, checking just in time the bitter laughter that was threatening to rise inside his throat again. They did not answer.

"Well?" he challenged. "Why should I want to?"

"To help your race live," answered the shorter one emotionlessly. "That's the only reason that will work. If you don't want that, then we've been wasting our time here—and time is precious."

He stopped speaking and gazed at Miles. Now it was

39

Miles' turn to feel that they were waiting for him to say something. But he did not know what to say.

"If you don't want to be your people's representative in the fight against the Horde," said the shorter one, slowly and deliberately as if he were spelling matters out for Miles, "you should tell us now, and we will leave."

Miles stared at him.

"You mean"—Miles looked narrowly at him—"you wouldn't choose somebody else?"

"There's no one else to choose," said the shorter one. "No one, that is, who'd be worth our time to work with. If you don't want to go, we'll leave."

"Wait," said Miles, as the two turned away. They stopped and turned back again.

"I didn't say I wouldn't," said Miles. "It's just that I don't understand anything about all this. Don't I have a right to have it explained to me first?"

"Of course," answered the taller one unexpectedly. "Ask us whatever you want to know."

"All right," said Miles. "What makes me so different from everybody else in the world, to make you pick me?"

"You have a capability for identification with all the other people in your world," answered the short one, "that is far greater than that of anyone else alive on that world at this present moment."

"Understand, we don't say," put in the taller one, "that at the present moment you've got this identification. We only mean that the capacity, the potential to have it, is in you. With our help that potential can be developed. You can step forward in this ability to a point your own race won't reach for many generations from now, under ordinary conditions."

"Your race's representative against the Horde has to have this identification," said the shorter one. "Because you're going to need to draw upon their sources of"—he hesitated, and then went on—"of something that they each possess so far only in tiny amounts. You must combine these tiny amounts in yourself, into something large enough so that you can effectively operate the type of weapon we will be giving you to use against the Horde."

He stopped speaking. For a moment Miles' mind churned with the information that had been given him. It sounded sensible—but he felt unexpectedly stubborn.

"How do I know this is all going to be for the benefit of human beings anyway?" he asked. "How do I know that it's not a case of our not being in danger at all—but your needing me and whatever this thing is that everybody has a little bit of just for your own purposes?"

Their faces did not change as they gazed at him.

"You'll have to trust us on that point," said the taller one quietly.

"Tell me one thing then," said Miles, challenging him. "Do you really look just like human beings?"

"No," said the smaller one, and the word seemed to echo and reecho in the room. "We put on this appearance the way you might put on a suit of clothes."

"I want to see you the way you actually are," said Miles.

"No," said the shorter one again. "You would not like what you saw if we showed you ourselves as we are."

"I don't care," said Miles. He frowned. "I'm an artist. I'm used to looking at things objectively. I'll make it a point not to let whatever you look like bother me."

"No," repeated the shorter one, still calmly. "You think you wouldn't let it bother you. But it would. And your emotional reaction to us would get in the way of your working with us against the Horde, whether or not you believe it now."

"Fine! I have to trust you!" said Miles grimly. "But you don't trust me!"

"Trust us or not," said the taller one. "If your world contributes a representative to the galaxy's defense, that will entitle it to whatever protection all our galaxy's defensive forces can give it. But your contribution is tiny. In the civilization from which we two come anyone, such as I or my friend here, can operate many weapons like the one you'll be given to handle. In short, one of our people has fighting abilities worth many times that of the total population of your world. So to us it's a small matter whether you join us or not. Your help counts—because the slightest additional bit of strength may be enough to swing the balance of power between the Horde and ourselves. But it is small to us, no matter how big it seems to you."

"In short," put in the smaller one, "to us you represent a fraction of a single individual defender like myself against the Horde. To yourself, you represent several billions of your people. The choice is up to you."

"If we're just one isolated little world, way out here," said Miles, with the uneasy suspicion that he was clutching at straws, "and not worth much, why should the Horde bother with us at all? If there are so many of you worth so much more in toward the center of the galaxy?"

"You have no understanding of the numbers and rapacity of the Horde," said the smaller one. "Suppose we show you a picture."

Instantly the room was gone from around Miles. He stood in the midst of dirt and rock—an eroded desert stretching to the horizon. Nowhere was there an intelligent creature, an animal—or even any sign of a bush, or tree, or plant. There was nothing—nothing but the raw surface of a world.

Suddenly he was back in the room again.

"That is what a world looks like after the Silver Horde has passed," said the shorter one. "That was a picture taken by those few who survived of the race that held the center of this galaxy before us, several million years ago. The Horde broke through then and processed everything organic for food. Its numbers are beyond your imagining. We could give you a figure, but it would have no real meaning for you."

"But," said Miles suddenly and sharply, "if the Horde came through the last time and cleaned off all the worlds like that which had life on them, how is it there are records like this?"

"We've never said that all of the galaxy's worlds would be ravaged by the Horde," said the taller one. "Some small percentage will escape by sheer chance. Even if we fight and lose, some of the ships that oppose them will escape, even from battle with the Horde. And these will begin to populate the galaxy again. So it was the last time, a million of your years ago, when the Horde came through. Those who lived here before us in the galaxy's center met them, as we will meet them, and fought them and lost. For a million years after that, the Horde fed its numbers on the living worlds of our galaxy until the pickings became so lean they were forced to move on. But as I say, some ships eluded them. Here and there a world was missed. After the Horde had passed, civilization began over again."

"And in the millions of years that have passed since," said the other, "even the ravaged worlds began to recover. Look at that same world again, the one we showed you. See it as it is today."

Once more Miles found himself standing in some other place than in the room at the Pentagon. Only, about him now were hills covered with a species of grass and a type of tall, twisted tree. Distantly, there were sounds as of small birds chittering, and something small and almost too fast for him to see scurried through the grasslike ground cover perhaps thirty feet from where he stood. Then, abruptly, he was back in the room again, facing the two aliens.

"All through the galaxy you will find worlds like that," said the shorter. "Their temperature and atmosphere and the rest of their physical makeup make them entirely inhabitable. But their flora and fauna are primitive, as if it had only been less than a billion years since they cooled from the whirlpool of coalescing stellar dusts and fragments that they were originally. But they are not that young. They've simply started over again, from the minute life of their oceans, since the Horde passed."

"Worlds like that will be available for settlement by your people if you survive the Horde," said the taller one.

"But even if I go, you say I may make no difference in stopping the Horde," said Miles. "And if I stay, our world may be one of those that the Horde somehow misses, anyway."

"This is perfectly true," said the smaller one. They both looked at him impassively. "But as I said earlier, our time is precious. You'll have to give us your answer now."

Miles turned and looked out the bedroom window, which also looked onto the small strip of grass of the interior courtyard. Beyond the strip of grass was a bare concrete wall. He looked at that and saw nothing on it—no mark, no shape. It was nothing but a featureless wall.

Equally blank was the reaction he felt within him toward the rest of the world. In spite of what Marie had said, in spite of what these aliens seemed to think, it was not people that mattered to him—but painting.

And then, leaping out of nowhere as if to clutch at his throat and stop his breathing, came a sudden understanding. If his world were wiped out, if his race were destroyed, what would become of his painting?

Suddenly it pounced upon Miles, like a lion from the underbrush, the realization that it was not merely the continuance of his work that was at stake here, but the very possibility of that work's existing at all. If he should stay here and paint, refusing to go with these two, and then the Horde came by to wipe out his world, and his paintings with it, what good would any of his painting have done? He had no choice. He had to defend the unborn ghosts of his future canvases, even at the risk of never being able to paint them.

He turned sharply to the two aliens.

"All right," he said. "I'm with you."

"Very well," said the shorter one. Miles' acceptance had not altered the expressions of their faces or the tones of their voices, any more than anything else he had said or done.

"What do I do then?" asked Miles. "I suppose we go to your ship?"

"We are already in the ship," said the shorter one. "We've been in it ever since you agreed to join us."

Miles looked about him. The room was unchanged. Beyond the little window, the strip of lawn and the far wall of the interiur courtyard was unchanged. He turned to see the two aliens moving out of the bedroom into the living room of the suite. He followed them and stopped short. The two Treasury agents were gone, and where there had been a door to the Pentagon corridor there was only wall now. The aliens waited while he stared about him.

"You see?" said the shorter one, after a moment.

"There's no door," Miles said stupidly.

"We don't use doors," said the aliens. "Soon, neither will you. This suite will be yours until we deliver you to the

Battle Line. Now, if you'll come back into the bedroom, we will begin your development."

Once more they led the way back into the bedroom. They stopped by the bed.

"And now," said the shorter one, "please lie down on your back on the bed."

Miles did so.

"Please close your eyes."

Miles did so. He lay there with his eyes closed, waiting for further orders. Nothing happened. After what seemed only a second he opened them again. The two aliens were gone.

Outside the bedroom window, night darkness held the courtyard. Darkness was also in the bedroom and filling the aperture of the half-open door to the sitting room. In spite of the fact that he seemed merely to have closed his eyes for a moment, he had a confused impression that some large length of time had passed. An impulse came to him to get up and investigate the situation, but at the very moment that it came to him, it slipped away again. A heavy sort of languor crept over him, a soothing weariness, as if he were at the end of some long day of hard physical effort. He felt not only weary, but also comforted. Dimly, he was aware that some great change had taken place in him, but he was too much at ease on the bed, soaked and steeped in his weariness, to investigate now what had happened.

Above all, he felt wrapped in peace. A great silent song of comfort and reassurance seemed to be enfolding him, buoying him up—lifting him up, in fact, like the crest of a wave on an endlessly, peacefully rocking ocean. He mounted the crest and slid slowly down into the next trough. The darkness moved in on him. He gave himself up to the rocking comfort.

Slowly consciousness slipped away from him, and he felt himself falling into a deep but natural sleep.

When he woke a second time, it was once more daylight, or its equivalent, beyond the windows of his bedroom. Daylight—not red, as the daylight had been since the moment of his painting on the river, but cheerful yellow daylight—filled the interior courtyard via the skylight. He looked around the room and saw the two aliens standing side by side not far from the bed, watching him.

Slowly he became conscious of himself. He felt strangely different, strangely light and complete. So lacking in the normal little pressures and sensations was he that he glanced down to see if his body was still there.

It was. He lay on the bed, wrapped or dressed in some sort of metallically glinting silver clothing that fitted him closely, covering all but his hands and his face. His body had never felt this way before. Nor his mind, for that matter. His head was so clear, so free of drowsiness and dullness and all the little hangovers of human tiredness, that his thoughts seemed to sing within it. He looked again at the two aliens.

"You can get up now," said the smaller.

Miles sat up, swung his legs over the side of the bed, and rose to his feet. The sensation of his rising was indescribable. It was almost as if he floated to his feet without muscular effort. As he stood facing the two aliens, the feeling of lightness in his body persisted. He felt, although his feet were flat on the floor, as if he were standing on tiptoe, with no effort involved.

"What's happened to me?" he asked wonderingly.

"You are now completely healthy. That's all," said the taller alien. "Would you like to take a look at yourself?"

Mike nodded.

He had barely completed the nod when the wall behind the two aliens suddenly became a shimmering mirror surface. He saw himself reflected in it, standing beside the bed wrapped in his close-fitting silver clothes, and for a moment he did not recognize himself.

The man who stood imaged in the mirror was erect and straight-limbed and looked bigger—bigger all over in some strange way—than Miles had remembered his mirror image's ever looking before. But it was not this so much that caused Miles to catch his breath. There was something drastically different about him now. Something had happened. He stared at himself for a long moment without understanding, and then he saw it. And an icy feeling of excitement ran down his spine.

46

In the tight silver sleeve that enclosed it to the wrist, his left arm was as large and full-muscled as his right. And the hand that terminated it was in no way different from the healthy hand at the end of his right arm.

Miles stood staring at it. He could not believe what he saw. And then—he could believe it, but he was afraid that if he looked away from it for an instant, what he saw would evaporate into a dream. Or what he saw would go back to being the way it had been these last six years. But he continued to stand there, and his mirrored image did not change. Slowly, almost dazedly, he turned his eyes to the two aliens.

"My arm," he said.

"Of course," said the small alien.

Miles turned back to the mirror surface. Hesitantly he lifted his good right arm to feel the left hand and arm. They were solid and warm, alive and movable, under the fingertips of what had been his lone good hand. A bubble of joy and amazement began to swell within him. He turned once more to the aliens.

"You didn't tell me about this," he said. "You didn't tell me my arm would be fixed."

"It was of a piece with the rest," said the taller alien. "And we did not want you to commit yourself because of anything like a bribe."

Miles turned back to the mirror surface, feeling his left arm and marveling at it once more. The sensation in the arm as he moved it woke him to the sensations of the rest of his body. Looking at himself closely in the mirror surface now, he saw that he was heavier, more erect, in every way stronger and more vital than he had been before. In his mind he tried to find words to express how it was with him now, but the words would not come. He felt all in one piece—and he felt invisible. That was the closest he could come to it. There were no sensations of sublevel pains, weariness, or heaviness about him. He and his body were one, as—he could now remember—he had not felt since he had been very young. He turned back to the aliens.

"Thank you," he said.

"There is no need to thank us," said the shorter of the two aliens. "What we did to you we did as much for ourselves as for you. Now it's time for you to start to become charged with the identification sense of your fellow humans."

Miles stared at him with interest.

"Shall I lie down on the bed again?" Miles asked.

"No," said the taller alien. "This next is nothing we can do for you. You have to do it all yourself. You've been away from the surface of your world for two and a half days now. During that time the people of your world have been informed through all possible news media that soon you'll be back and moving about among them. They've been told, if they see you, not to speak to you or show any awareness of you. They're simply to let you wander among them and treasure up in their minds the sight of you."

"That's all I do?" demanded Miles.

"Not quite all," said the smaller of the two. "You have to open your inner consciousness to their sense of identification with you and what you'll be doing in their name. You must endeavor to feel toward them as they feel toward you. You must learn to consider them precious."

"But where do I go first? What should I do?" Miles asked.

"Simply—wander," the shorter alien said. "Do you know a poem called *The Rime of the Ancient Mariner*? Written by a man named Coleridge."

"I've read it," said Miles.

"Then perhaps you remember the lines with which the Ancient Mariner explains his moving about the Earth to tell his story," said the smaller one. There still was no perceptible emotion in his voice, but as he quoted the two lines that followed, it seemed that they rang with particular emphasis in Miles' mind and memory.

> . . . I pass, like night, from land to land;
> I have strange power of speech. . . .

"You will find," the smaller of the two aliens went on, "that it'll be with you as it was with the poem's Ancient Mariner. If you want to move from one place to another, you only need to think of the place you want to be, and you will be there. If you want to lift yourself into the air

48

or fly like a bird, you can do it by thinking of it. You'll find that no lock will be able to keep you out of any place you want to enter. No wall will bar you. If you wish, you can walk through any barrier. The people of your world who can be reached by the news media have been warned to expect this. They have been told to expect you anywhere—even in their own homes. They have been asked to cooperate by ignoring you when you appear suddenly among them."

"What if they don't ignore me?" asked Miles. "Your asking them to do it doesn't guarantee they will."

"Those who don't ignore you," said the taller alien, "won't be offering you the necessary identification you are out to gather from as many of your race as possible. So remove yourself from the presence of anyone who does not cooperate, because you will be wasting your time. As far as any inimical actions are concerned, you'll find that while you can touch anything you like, you can't be touched or hurt by anything, unless you wish it—right up to and including your race's nuclear weapons. Nothing can hold you, and nothing can harm you."

He fell silent. Miles stood uncertainly for a moment.

"Well," he said at last. "Shall I go now, then, and start?"

"The sooner, the better," said the taller alien. "Simply think of the spot on the surface of the Earth where you want to be and you'll be there."

"And when shall I come back?" asked Miles.

"When you've gathered together an identification sense with enough of your fellow humans, you'll know it," said the shorter alien. "Simply decide then to come back here to the ship and you'll be here. Then we'll leave together for the defense line that's being set up outside the spiral arm of the galaxy to meet the Silver Horde."

"All right," said Miles slowly. He felt strange. It was as if everything that had happened to him had happened within a few moments. At the same time, he was surprised to feel that he was not overwhelmed by it all. Now, particularly since he was in this rebuilt, newly perfect body, all that the aliens said seemed entirely natural, and all that he had to do seemed entirely normal.

He wondered where on Earth it would be best to go to

first. While he was still wondering, a stray impulse made him look once more into the mirror image of the wall. He saw himself there, and he could not help smiling at what he saw. He turned back to the aliens.

"I'm a new man, all right," he said to them.

For the first time since he had met them, Miles saw one of them shake his head. It was the shorter alien.

"No," said the shorter alien. Neither of them was smiling back. "You're not a *new* man. You're Everyman."

5

He had been puzzling over the point at which he wished to arrive first on his return to Earth, but at the last minute it proved to be no trouble whatsoever. Like the point of a compass needle drawn toward the magnetic north, he found himself suddenly on the steps of the dormitory where Marie lived. It was night about him. On the street running through the campus the streetlights were lit, and the head lights of cars flickered past through the high shrubbery that shielded the dormitory grounds from the street itself. On each side of the row of glass doors that gave entrance to the building, a tall lamp glowed yellowly. He walked up and through the doors into the lobby.

As he entered, he saw that the lounge beyond the desk was empty. He went to the desk itself. On duty was the same small girl with dark glasses and a pointed face who had been on duty the last time he had called here for Marie. She glanced at him for a second as he came in, then quickly glanced away again, down at her desk below the counter, where some textbooks and a notebook were spread out. She kept her eyes on the textbooks as he came up. He stopped at the counter and leaned over it.

"I know it must be late," he said. "But this is a sort of emergency. Would you ring Marie Bourtel's room for me, please?"

She did not answer, and she did not move. He saw her profile, just a couple of feet from him, bent rigidly above an open textbook. There was a faint shine on her forehead as of perspiration—and suddenly he realized that she was following directions. She was ignoring him, even to the point of not looking at him or replying to him when he spoke directly to her.

He sighed, a little heavily. All at once, he seemed to sense the quality of her fear. It came through to him like the faint rapid beating of a bird's heart, felt as the bird is held in the hand. It occurred to him that he could probably turn and go up the stairs to Marie's room. Then he had a better thought. He looked at the board of numbers that hung beyond the little clerk, with a hook beneath each number and keys on some of the hooks. Above each hook was a name. He sought out Marie's name, noted that the hook held no key, and looked for the number below the hook. Marie's room number jumped at him. It was forty-six. That would mean she was on the fourth floor. Now that he stopped to think of it, he remembered her mentioning she was on the fourth floor.

He concentrated on the hook and closed his eyes for a second. When he opened them, he stood in darkness in a small room. The blind on the single window was drawn nearly all the way. Below it the window had been raised a little, and the white curtains waved sleepily in the soft inrush of cool night air. The girls in the dormitory were normally assigned two to a room, but Marie, as a counselor, had a room to herself. Looking about, he saw her now, a still figure under the covers of the bed in one corner of the room.

He walked softly over toward her and looked down at her sleeping face. She slept on her side, her pale features in profile against the white pillow and her hair spread out behind them upon it. One hand was up on the pillow beside her face.

"Marie," he said softly.

She did not waken. He repeated her name a little louder.

This time she stirred. Her hand drew back down under the covers, but her eyes did not open. He reached out one hand to the switch of the bedside lamp on the small table only a foot or so from her face. Then he changed his mind, and his hand drew back. To waken her to the sudden glare of the lamp seemed too much of a shock.

He looked over at the slight rectangle below the shade where the window was open. An inspiration came over

51

him. He thought of the light, the pale light coming in through that opening, as gathering and strengthening in the room, and as he watched, it built up around them. Either that—or his eyes became accustomed to the dimness—he was not quite sure which.

"Marie," he said, bending over and murmuring directly into her ear.

She stirred again, and this time her eyes blinked and then sleepily opened. For a moment they stared at him without recognition, and then they flew wide.

Her head lifted, and her mouth opened. For a moment he thought that she had not recognized him after all: that she had taken him for some intruder and was about to scream. But before he could put his hand over her mouth, her mouth closed, and she lay back again, staring up at him with almost fearful eyes filled with the shadow of the darkened room.

"Miles . . ." she whispered on a long slow breath.

"Marie," he said. He bent over and kissed her. And her arms went up and around his neck, at first softly and then fiercely holding him. For a moment they clung together, and then he drew back, loosening her arms but holding her hands with his own hands as he sat down on the edge of the bed.

"Marie," he whispered. "Never mind what you've been hearing people on Earth should do. Talk to me."

"Yes, Miles," she said, and her mouth curved in a slow, oddly tender smile. "You came here to me," she said.

"I had to accept, Marie," he said. "I had to agree to do what they asked."

"I know," she murmured, looking at him through the dimness. "Oh, Miles! You came to me!"

"I had to see you first," Miles said, still holding her hands. "I wanted you to know all about it, before I"—he hesitated—"went ahead."

She lay looking at him in the faint but pervasive light from the slightly opened window which he had increased.

"What're you going to do now?" she asked him.

"I don't know," he said. "What I'm supposed to do, I guess. Roam around the world and see if I pick up some kind of charge from the people I meet and see."

Her hands tightened on his.

"How long will you do that?" she asked softly.

"I don't know," he answered. "The aliens said I'd know when I was ready. According to them, I don't think it's supposed to take too long. They kept talking about the fact that time was precious."

"Maybe you shouldn't be here talking with me then," she said, but her hands held as tightly to him as ever.

"Maybe not," he echoed. And strangely, once he had said it, the feeling of urgency began to grow inside him, as if somewhere within himself he contained the knowledge that time indeed 'was precious: the knowledge that he must not waste it, as he was wasting it now.

"I guess I've got to go," he said. He released his fingers from her grip, which held tightly for a second more and then let him go.

"But you'll come back?" she asked, as he stood up beside the bed. He saw her face, by the trick of the shadow in the room seeming to lie far below him instead of merely an arm's length away.

"I'll come back," he answered.

"I don't mean before you leave," she said quickly. "I mean afterward. You'll come back safely?"

"I'll come back safely, all right," he said. And with the words a strange, bright, animallike anger seemed to kindle inside him, a deep, white-hot atavistic fury, a determination that he would come back—in spite of anything.

He bent over and kissed her once more, then released the arms she had locked around his neck and stood erect again.

"Good-bye," he said and willed himself to be back once more on the sidewalk before the dormitory.

Instantly he was there.

He turned and walked off a little from the light of the entrance into the shadow of the Norway pines lining the driveway. He wondered what to do first. Where to go? With all the world to choose from, he found himself confused by the countless number of places he might visit. Finally, he threw it all from his mind and chose at random. He had never been to Japan. He thought of Tokyo.

Abruptly, he was there. It was bright morning. He stood on a crowded street, and passersby flowed about him as if he were a rock in a stream. The buildings were all

Western-looking. The people he saw were all in Western dress. Only the rattle of their voices, sounding high-pitched and unfamiliar, gave a touch of strangeness to the scene. Then it was as if his mind had broken through a thin film like a soap bubble that enclosed him—and he found himself understanding what they were saying.

He stood listening and watching those who came by for any reaction to his appearance there, dressed in his strange silver suit. But although eyes glanced at him, they glanced away again. For a moment he was astonished that the response of the people in the world should be so strongly conditioned by the instructions of the aliens. And then something that came to him by the same route as his understanding of the Japanese words being spoken around him told him that it was as much politeness as anything else that was keeping the gaze of those about him from lingering on him. He began to walk down the street.

As he did, he began to lose his self-consciousness. The understanding and communication he seemed to be holding with the people about him, just below the level of consciousness, grew stronger as he passed among them. He was conscious of *feeling* their presence about him, as if some hidden radarlike eye was registering their presence over and above the impressions of sight and sound and smell that touched his senses. It was like something felt and something heard. As he opened himself to it, he felt it like a great, soft, sad roar of sound, a sort of voiceless music reflecting the character and the spirit of the people about him.

The flavor of that soundless sound, that inner feeling that flowed from them as a group, reached in and touched him deeply. And now that he devoted his attention to it, he began to distinguish—in a sense, to touch—individual threads in the pattern. Threads that were individual emotional responses or empathies—he did not know the right word for whatever they might be, but he felt them like living things under his fingers. Also, now that he had picked out these individual feelings, he could feel that from each one he touched in this manner he himself gained a little bit. From each one he learned something; he was in some way a little stronger.

So this was what it was like—the "charging" process

54

that the aliens had mentioned.

On impulse, he switched to Peking. Here the people were dressed differently, and the streets were different in appearance—and the people did not ignore him but came crowding around him. But here, too, he encountered the feeling again. Again there was a totality that was different—a group difference, but within this, making it up as it were, were the individual characteristics from which he took something to add to himself.

But here the attention was all on him, and he was not gaining as much from those who surrounded him. Their hands reached out to him, and though their fingers slipped off him as if he were encased in glass, very little of the learning process came through to him from them. He closed his eyes and willed himself to another Chinese scene that he had seen once in a traveler's photograph.

When he opened his eyes, he stood on top of a huge block of stone—a miniature mountain several hundred feet high. About him were other miniature mountains, rising from a flat landscape, with peaceful small lakes and quiet, small green islands at their foot. It was like a giant's toyscape all about him. Below, moving in rows across a flooded rice field, he could see the bent backs of people at work. And from them and from all of the scene around and to the horizon came much more strongly the group feeling he had now encountered twice before. Here they were not aware of him, and he felt himself drawing knowledge and strength from them as the sun sucks up moisture from the surface of a body of water.

But after a while he began to reach the limit of that absorption. His mind took him to London, to a street down which he had walked on a trip several years before—a street entering Piccadilly Circus. It was Regent Street, and the pale light of dawn was just beginning to wash the faces of the buildings along its curving length. There were few people about, but from these he received strongly and clearly. Again, again, again—always what he felt or tasted or heard within him was different. But now he knew what he was looking for, and from this point he began his pilgrimage about this world of his birth.

He roamed it, his world, from a Spanish hillside to a Yukon lumbering camp, from the mountains of Mexico to the streets of Brasilia, to Cape Town, to the African jungle, to Bokhara, to Moscow and the Russian steppes.

He walked down the streets of Helsinki. He drifted in the thin air above the sharp mountains that divide Genoa from Milan. He skimmed a few feet above fishing craft in the blue harbors of the north Mediterranean shore. Daylight and dark, all the hours of light and shade and weather and seasons flickered about him, like the changing slides of scenes shown on a screen by a slide projector. And gradually these scenes blended together. Light and dark, north and south, land and sea, winter and summer, yellow, black, brown and white and red—all peoples, all places, and all times wove themselves into a tapestry of feeling that was the overfeeling of the people of Earth and of Earth itself.

But by the time he had achieved this tapestry of feeling some days had passed. He floated once more, at last, above the point where the Mississippi and the Minnesota rivers joined and the twin cities of St. Paul and Minneapolis lay together. This had been his starting place. He was aware now for the first time that since his beginning—how many days ago?—he had not felt any need for food or drink or sleep. The only need he had felt was the need that had grown in him to know and understand the people he surveyed. Now it was almost done.

He had grown in knowledge in his traveling. He understood now what he had felt in a cruder sense when he had first realized that if the Horde destroyed the world, his paintings might as well never have been painted. He felt a strong thread now—not thread, cord, for it was woven of all the threads of feeling he had gathered from individuals about the Earth—connecting anything he did with the people of Earth.

In a sense, everything that was made or done by any member of the human race belonged to the race. This was something he had never understood before. But, he reminded himself now, Marie had known it—or at least she had sensed it and had tried to tell him that night of the day in which the sun had turned red.

It was Marie he wanted to see just once more before returning to the ship and whatever waited for him at the hands of the two Center Aliens.

It was night—as it had been when he had seen her last. Hanging in midair below a few scattered gray clouds, under a nearly full moon, and some three hundred feet above the meeting of the rivers and the green river bottom, he turned toward the buildings of the campus, which even at this distance were visible in the moonlight. He willed himself once more into Marie's room.

As before, it was late and she was asleep, one hand up on the pillow beside her face. He stepped to the bedside and stood looking down. He felt an impulse to speak to her. But something checked him.

He stood looking down at her in the night dimness of the room. Slowly he began to understand why he had checked. The tapestry, that woven cord of identification with all the people he had passed among in the last number of days, was something that did not allow him an individual connection with some single person anymore. As the shorter alien had said to him before he left the ship, he was not Miles Vander any longer—he was Everyman.

But if he came back alive, things would be different. He would be Miles Vander once more. And Marie would still be here.

His time was up. He looked away from Marie and, lifting his head, looked in his mind's eye out to the alien spaceship.

In that moment, he was there.

He stood in the living room of the suite that he had first entered in the Pentagon. The two aliens stood facing him.

"I'm ready now," he told them.

"That's good," answered the shorter one. "Because time is short."

He waved a hand at one wall of the room. Miles looked at it or through it—he was not sure which—and saw the sun, changing back as he watched from its red to a normal yellow color, and below it the Earth, blue under that yellow light. As he watched, the blue globe that was the Earth began to shrink. It shrank rapidly, dwindling into the blackness of star-filled space around it.

Abruptly, all space began to move. The lights of the stars lengthened and became streaks. They became fine bars of light extending in both directions.

"Where to now?" asked Miles.

"To our defense line, beyond the spiral arm of the galaxy," answered the shorter alien.

Even as he spoke, Miles felt a sudden sense of disorientation—a strange feeling as if, in less than no time at all, he had suddenly been wrenched apart, down to the component parts of his very atoms, and spread out over inconceivable distances, before being, in the same infinitesimal moment, reassembled at some far distant place.

"First shift," commented the taller alien. "At the best we can do there will be five more like that, with necessary time for calculation between."

It did indeed require five more such moments of disorientation called shifts to complete their journey. Miles came to understand that in that moment of disorientation the ship and all within it changed position across many light-years of distance. But having jumped suddenly in this manner from one point to another, it was forced to stop and recalculate, even though its calculators were awesome by human standards, for a matter of hours or days before it could establish its due position and figure the position toward which it would next shift. All in all, it took what Miles estimated to be something like a week and a half of interior time aboard the ship before they finally reached the defense line toward which they were heading.

They came out not at the line itself but some hours of cruising time away. This, Miles was given to understand by the shorter alien, was because of the safety factor required in the calculation of a shift. For a shift brought them only approximately to the destination they had figured, and to calculate without a margin of safety might mean coming out in the space occupied by some other solid body—with a resultant explosion that would have been to a nuclear explosion as a nuclear explosion is to that of a firecracker.

As it was, it took several hours of driving through curiously starless space before Miles began to pick out what seemed to be a star, a single star, far ahead of them.

As they grew close to this, however, it began to take on the disk shape and yellow color of a sun, like the sun of Earth.

"No," said the shorter alien, standing beside Miles in the large, almost featureless room with the large screen which seemed to be the pilot room of the aliens' ship. Miles looked at him. Miles was becoming used to having his thoughts answered as if he had spoken them aloud.

"It's not a real star," went on the smaller alien. "It's an artificial sun—a lamp we've set up here to light our Battle Line for us when we meet the Horde."

"Where's the defense line?" Miles asked.

"It ought to be in view in a few minutes," answered the shorter alien.

Miles turned to look at the other. In spite of the change that had taken place in him, and in spite of the fact they had been together aboard the ship now for some days, he had gotten no feeling of response from the two aliens. It was as if they were wrapped around, not merely with human appearances, but with some sort of emotional and mental protective device that kept him from feeling them the way he had felt the people of his own world, as individuals. It struck Miles now that from the first he had had no names for the two of them. They had simply been the taller and the shorter, in his mind, and whenever he had spoken to one, the one at whom he directed his words seemed instinctively to know he had the responsibility to answer.

"What are you people like, in there toward the center of the galaxy?" Miles asked now, looking down at the other. "I don't think I ever asked you." The alien did not turn his head but kept gazing into the screen as he answered.

"There's nothing I can tell you," he said. "You are, as I said, a barbarian by our standards. Even if I could explain us to you, you wouldn't understand. Even if you could understand what we're like, knowing it would only frighten and disturb you."

A little anger stirred in Miles at this answer. But he held it down.

"Don't tell me you know everything, you people?" he asked.

"Not everything," answered the alien. "No. Of course not."

"Then there's always the chance that you might be mistaken about me, isn't there?" said Miles.

"No," said the alien flatly.

He did not offer any further explanation. Miles, to keep

his anger under control, made himself drop the subject. He turned back to watching the screen. After some minutes, during which the orb of the distant sunlike lamp continued to swell until it was very nearly the size of the sun as seen from Earth, he began to catch sights of glints of reflected light forming a rough bar across the lower part of the screen.

"Yes," said the alien beside him, once more answering his unspoken question. "You're beginning to see part of the ships, the supply depots, and all else that make up our defense line."

As they got even closer, the line began to reveal itself as visible structures. But even then, Miles discovered, the screen could not hold any large part of it in one picture. With a perception he suddenly discovered he now possessed, Miles estimated the line to stretch at least as far as the distance from the solar system's sun to its outermost planet.

They seemed to be moving in toward the thickest part of the line, and as they got close, Miles saw round ships very much like the one he was on. These floated in space, usually with a raftlike structure nearby, and were spaced at regular intervals across the screen.

Miles had assumed that they were fairly close by this time. But to his intense surprise they continued to drive onward at a good speed, and the ships continued to swell on the screen before him. It was some seconds before he realized that the ships they were approaching were truly titanic in size, as large in proportion to the ship he was on as the ship he was on would have been to a four-engine commercial jet of Miles' native Earth. These great ships were certainly no less than several thousand miles in diameter.

"If you want a word for them," the alien beside Miles answered his unspoken thought, "you might call them our dreadnought class of fighting vessels. Actually, they're not fighting vessels the way you'd think of them at all. They're only vehicles to carry a certain critical number of our own people, who will use their personal weapons on the Horde when the Horde gets within range. Without our people inside it, that ship you see is a simple shell of metal and not much more."

It was becoming clear to Miles that they were headed for one monster of a ship in particular. He assumed they would be transferring him into the larger ship and wondered what it would be like inside that enormous shell of metal. But instead of coming right up to the dreadnought, they slowed and stopped in space perhaps four or five miles from its surface. At first Miles did not understand this. Then, turning around, he discovered he was alone in the room. His wide-ranging awareness, developed during those last days on Earth, echoed back the information to him that he was now alone on this ship. Plainly, the two aliens had gone to the larger vessel to report or whatever their duty required them to do.

It was some minutes before either returned, and then only one came back. It was the taller of the two who finally materialized alone in the pilot room of the ship, where Miles was waiting, and Miles' awareness told him that the two of them were alone in the ship.

"I'll take you now to your position on the line," said the taller alien. As usual, he did nothing that Miles could see with his hands; but the unbroken surface of the dreadnought filling most of the screen began to slide off it at one side, and Miles knew that they were moving away from it and down the Battle Line toward its left end.

If the dreadnought had proved to be larger than Miles had ever imagined, the distance to the left end of the line from its middle turned out to be even longer than he had estimated. For several hours they slid at high speed past globe-shaped vessels of varying size, from the enormous bulk of the dreadnought down to the ships smaller than the one Miles was on. As they approached the far end of the line, the ships grew progressively smaller. Also, their shape changed. No longer were they all globular. Many of them were rod- or cigar-shaped.

"These are the ships," the taller alien explained to Miles, without being asked, "of those outlying races that prefer to fight in their own way and with the ships they have built themselves and with which they are familiar. Because they're effective, we let them do this. You, and those you'll be joining, will fight in ships and weapons we supply."

There was something chilling about this pronounce-

61

ment. Miles had not grown close to either of the two Center Aliens, but if he had felt closer to one than another, it had been the shorter instead of the taller. The taller one had always seemed more remote and less approachable than the smaller alien. Now that remoteness came through to Miles with extra force. Miles felt as a speck of dust might feel, lectured by a mountain. He was not being given a choice—he was only being given orders.

In silence they moved on, until the ships dwindled to the point of being very small indeed, until, finally, the point was reached at which the ships, instead of hanging in space beside the raftlike structures which evidently held their supplies and material, were small enough to lie on those rafts. Still they went on, until they came at last to what seemed to be the end of the line.

Here, on a raft several times the size of a football field, lay a ship hardly bigger than a nuclear submarine of Earth. The larger ship holding Miles and the taller alien stopped perhaps half a mile from it.

"Now," said the taller alien—and without warning he and Miles were transported to the raft.

Miles found himself standing on a metal surface at the foot of a metal ladder leading up to an open doorway in the side of the ship. There was no visible shell about the raft to enclose a breathable atmosphere, yet he breathed. The doorway was dark, in contrast with the light outside from the distant sunlamp. Miles could not see what might be inside.

"This ship," said the taller alien quietly, "is the smallest of our scout ships. It is staffed by thirty individuals, each a representative of a world like your own. You will become the thirty-first—and last—individual to make up its crew. In the weeks to come, you, with the others, will learn to maneuver it and together use its weapon. Now follow me. I'll take you to join the rest of the crew."

The taller alien floated up the ladder. Miles, starting to float behind him, felt an unexpected spasm of stubbornness. Instead of levitating, he seized hold of the ladder and climbed it like an ordinary mortal.

As his head drew level with the entrance, he could see inside. The taller alien was waiting for him in what seemed to be a small room or hatchway with a further entrance beyond. Miles joined him, and the alien turned without a word to lead him through the interior hatchway into a large room furnished with chairs and tables of various sizes and dimensions. Miles walked after him into the light of the room—and stopped abruptly.

The room was full. On its furniture and around its walls stood and sat a variety of different-appearing beings. All were four-limbed, standing upright on the lower two and with handlike appendages at the end of their upper pair. They all were of roughly the same size and proportions and general shape. But there was tremendous variety.

No two had the same skin color. No two had the same facial appearance. All had roughly similar features, as far as possessing two eyes and a single nose and mouth was concerned. But from there on everything was different. Their appearance ranged from that of the completely innocuous to the completely ferocious—from one being who seemed as round and inoffensive as a toy bear to one who seemed a walking tiger, equipped with a pair of ripping teeth projecting from the upper jaw over his lower lip.

"Members of this ship," said the alien, stepping aside to let them all see Miles, "let me introduce you to your new fellow crew member, who on his own world is known as Miles Vander."

He spoke in a tongue which Miles had never heard before but which Miles found he understood, as he had earlier understood all the various languages of Earth.

He turned back to face Miles.

"I'll leave you in their hands," he said in English. And disappeared.

Miles looked around him.

Those of his new fellow crew members who had been seated about the room were now getting to their feet and moving forward. Those who had been on their feet were also moving forward.

"Well," said Miles, speaking in the language he had just heard, "I'm glad to meet you all."

There was no response. They continued to close in on him, making a tight circle with no space between any of them. Now he sensed it—with all his new sensitivity. There was an atmosphere in the room of savagery and bloodlust, of anticipation and fury. They closed in silently like wolves about a stranger wolf, the one with the tigerlike features moving in directly before Miles and directly toward him.

The tigerlike being came on. Even when the others stopped, now locked in a tight ring around Miles, he came on until he stood only at arm's length from Miles. And then he stopped.

"My name is Chak'ha!" he said. He spoke the common language in a growling, throaty combination of sounds that no human vocal apparatus could have originated or imitated, but Miles understood him perfectly.

And even as he said it, Chak'ha launched himself, clawlike nails outstretched, tusks gleaming, at Miles' throat, and Miles went down under the attack.

6

As he fell backward with the being called Chak'ha on top of him, Miles felt panic, like a cold jagged knife, ripping upward through his belly toward his throat.

For a moment he froze, staring up at the toothed face snarling down into his own. Then, out of something deep within him came a counteracting mingled fear and fury, as primitive and brutal as the attack on him. Suddenly he was fighting back.

It was a simple, instinctive, animallike battle. They rolled on the metal deck together, fighting, scratching, biting, and digging at each other with every nail, tooth, or bony extremity that could be used as a weapon. For some seconds, for Miles, there was nothing but this. He had awakened into an instinctive rage out of simple fear for his life. But just as the rage had followed fear, now something beyond rage followed again.

It came over him like drunkenness. Suddenly he found that he did not care what Chak'ha was doing to him as long as he was able to continue what he was doing to Chak'ha. The adrenalized passion of destruction filled and intoxicated him.

In a second all those meanings which the activities of his upper mind had given his life until now were washed away in the brutal impulses from the older centers of his brain. His response to the light and shape and beauty that was art left him. His deep bond with the rest of the human race, which he had forged before being brought to this place, was forgotten. So was Marie. All that was left was the deep, primeval urge to tear and kill.

He had his hands now around the thick-skinned, leathery throat of Chak'ha, his thumbs digging in. Chak'ha's saber teeth and claws were slashing him wildly, but he felt no pain—he was only dimly aware of the blood running from his many wounds. *Die! Die!* his mind shouted at the alien as he tried to tighten his grip on the other's windpipe, wherever in that thick neck it might be.

. . .

But Chak'ha was not dying. He was continuing to slash at Miles—and gradually Miles began to realize that his own grip was weakening. All at once he became aware that he was losing blood too fast. He was failing.

A cold inner wind blew suddenly across his hot passion for killing. It was not the alien who was in danger of dying—it was himself. Something deeper than panic moved in him, and suddenly he remembered all that, for a moment, he had forgotten: Marie, the paintings he had yet to do, the people of his Earth. His grip was slipping weakly from Chak'ha's neck now—*but he could not afford to die!*

Without warning, for the second time in his life, he went into a state of hysterical strength.

Suddenly the tiger-faced alien was a toy in his hands. Chak'ha had already pulled loose from Miles' grip on his throat and half turned away. But Miles caught him again now easily. Miles turned him, slid one arm under Chak'ha's right armpit and the other under the alien's left armpit, then clasped his hands together behind the other's neck and pressed. Chak'ha's neck bent like a straw-filled tube of leather, and there came from it a creaking sound.

Abruptly, a strange gray fog seemed to fold itself about the mind and body of Miles. Dimly, he was aware that it was nothing his opponent had done. Nor was it anything that had been done by any of those standing in a tight circle around him and his enemy. It was something that seemed to come from the ship itself or from something beyond the ship.

Unexpectedly, the fires of his hysteria were smothered.

His muscles lost their strength. He was aware of his arms falling limply away, his fingers loosening and losing their grasp together behind Chak'ha's neck. Like a man under heavy sedation, he rolled off the back of his opponent and lay lost in the gray fog.

He was vaguely aware of the fact that Chak'ha, beside him, was also lying limply, wrapped in the same helpless condition. Above and around him, Miles was vaguely conscious of the circle of onlookers breaking up and drifting away. He saw a couple of them pick up the lax form of Chak'ha and carry it off. Alien hands also grasped him by the shoulders and legs and lifted him.

He felt himself being carried—where or to what, he was indifferent. He saw the ceiling of a corridor swaying above him; he saw the upper part of a doorway and then the ceiling of a smaller room. He felt himself thrown onto what seemed to be a soft surface, the soft undersurface of a niche in the wall that could be a bunk or a bed. Then he was left alone, and he slept.

When he woke at last, it was a gradual awakening. He felt that he had been asleep for some time that was not a short time. At first he felt nothing; then he became gradually conscious of his stiffness and the soreness that encompassed his whole body.

He still lay on the bunk on which he had been thrown. He lifted his head now to look at himself. Nothing, he could see, had been done for him. On the other hand the deep bites and scratches—in fact, all the injuries he had taken in his battle with Chak'ha—were already scabbed over and healing. He felt weak, but aside from this, and aside from the aches, which were no worse than those after a hard game of football as he remembered it from his junior high school days, he felt as good as ever.

He turned his head. Across the width of the small room from him, on another bunk, was the tiger-faced alien. Chak'ha was also awake and looking back at him. The other's two tusks glinted in the illumination from the lighting panel overhead, while the rest of the heavy body lay still half-hidden in the shadow of the bunk. It was impossible to read Chak'ha's expression, but even with the weakness and the aches, Miles felt gathering once more within him the white heat of that lustful joy of killing he

66

had experienced during the fight.

He grinned at Chak'ha challengingly. But the other dropped his own gaze, and abruptly Miles understood, partly through the sensitivity to the emotions of others that had been given him with his new body by the Center Aliens, but partly also through some likeness between him and Chak'ha that had nothing to do with the Center Aliens at all, that he had conquered at least this one of his fellow crewmen.

"Do you jump everybody who comes aboard here for the first time?" asked Miles.

Chak'ha lifted his gaze and answered. "No more," he said. "This boat is full now. You were the last. Now I'm last."

There was something odd about the meaning of the word of their strange common shipboard language which Chak'ha had used to give the meaning of "last" —something almost like a pun, a double meaning. It was as if Chak'ha said "last" but at the same time also gave it the meaning of "least." It was a subtle but undeniable connotation that Miles could not quite pin down, for the odd reason that he found he knew this strange language too well. He spoke it and translated it into English in his head at the same time. But he was not able to compare his translation with the actual sounds that he heard and that his own tongue and lips and throat made, for the reason that the knowledge that the Center Aliens had given him of this tongue was way down within him on the level of automatic verbal habit. He could no more hear with an unprejudiced ear the strange words he spoke than a man can hear with analytical detachment the accent with which he speaks his native tongue.

He shook his head a little and dropped the question of the double meaning.

"What do we do now, then?" he asked Chak'ha.

"Do?" answered Chak'ha. "Nothing. What's there to do?"

He dropped back on the bed and rolled over on his back, staring at the ceiling of his bunk.

There was a lifelessness, an air of defeat, to Chak'ha's answer. Puzzled but curious, Miles made an effort to get up. Wincing, he managed to get his legs over the edge of the bed and rise to his feet. He was stiff and sore but, he decided, certainly able with a little bit of willpower to make himself get around. He walked stiffly out of the small room and into the corridor outside.

Another member of the crew was passing. It was a round, bearlike alien. Miles stiffened, ready for anythng up to and including physical attack. But the rotund alien merely gave him the briefest and most incurious of glances and walked on. Miles turned to stare after him, then followed. Now would be as good a time as any to explore this vessel to which he had been assigned.

It was exactly that, in the next hour, which he did. Gradually he examined the vessel's interior from stem to stern. He also counted the rest of the members of the crew. Including himself, there seemed to be twenty-three, each one curiously different from the others.

But even more curious than these differences was the ship itself. Astonishingly, it seemed to have no power plant at all—beyond what might lie concealed in the small space below the console of the control panel in the bow room of the ship. Beyond this control room, which was set up for no more than three individuals to work in at one time, there were crew quarters, rooms with from one to as many as four bunks in them, the number of bunks seeming to vary without reason or purpose from room to room. There was the lounge, which he had first entered, taking up the large middle part of the ship and furnished with a number of different items of what he took to be furniture or recreational devices—among them, he was half-amused, half-embarrassed to see, was a very earthly overstuffed chair with a small, round coffee table alongside it.

Within the rest of the hollow cigar shape of the ship Miles discovered twenty of what looked like gun emplacements, ten on each side of the vessel.

In each one of these was what seemed to be a weapon, consisting of a gunner's seat joined to a heavy mechanism on a swivel. Handgrips flanked the mechanism on the side facing the gunner's seat, and on the far side there projected toward a bubble-shaped transparency what Miles at first took to be the equivalent of a gun barrel. But on closer examination, he found that it was not a hollow cylinder as any gun barrel with which he was familiar should be. It was a solid rod of metal, in the end of which he could discover not even the pinhole end of a passage for whatever force the weapon expelled.

Moreover, thought Miles, if the solid rods were indeed the equivalent of rifle barrels, whatever force they projected must pass harmlessly through the transparent bubble before them.—And if this was the case, why could not the Horde defend itself simply by using an equivalent of the transparent material as armor around its own ships?

There were too many questions for him to answer by himself. He needed help. So far the only one who had spoken to him at all had been Chak'ha. He turned back toward the room in which the tiger-faced alien lay on his bunk, but a feeling of wariness stopped him. Chak'ha was going no place. There would be ample time to ask him questions later. Perhaps, thought Miles, caution placing a hand on his shoulder, it would be to his advantage to see what he could deduce on his own before exposing his ignorance—even to the one other crew member he had conquered.

He went back to the lounge and sat down in the overstuffed chair he had noticed there earlier. The minute he seated himself the small coffee table beside him chimed softly, and silently, from nowhere that he could see, a cup of coffee materialized, black and steaming, sitting on a saucer in the center of the table.

Miles was not hungry. It came back to him forcefully now that he had not been hungry—had not in fact wanted any food at all—since the Center Aliens had first altered and improved him. But as the coffee cup appeared, he became conscious that at the back of his mind, as a sort of counterpoint to his bodily stiffness and soreness, he had been thinking about coffee out of habitual reflex. Curious now, he tested the table once more by thinking about a slice of apple pie. It, too, appeared on the table, beside the cup of coffee and with a fork on the plate that held it.

But when he picked the fork up to taste it, a globe of grayness, an opaqueness, formed abruptly about him. Suddenly he was unable to see anyone else in the room. A little alarmed, he put the fork down on the coffee table, and the opaqueness immediately cleared. He picked up the coffee cup, and once more the barrier to sight surrounded him.

With that, he understood.

He was to be given privacy while he ate. Either that, or his crewmates were to be protected from the sight of his eating. More likely, thought Miles, it was the latter.

He ate the pie and drank the coffee. As soon as they were emptied, the utensils which had held the pie and coffee disappeared from the coffee table. The opaqueness cleared from about Miles' chair, and he sat back to observe his crewmates as they passed through or rested in the lounge.

Within the next three or four hours, as he watched, fully three-quarters of the twenty-two other individuals he had counted aboard this ship passed before his eyes. Occasionally there were gray blurs in other parts of the room, as other crew members indulged in whatever eating or other habits were native to them. Outside of these occurrences, however, no one that Miles watched appeared to have anything particular to do or to be engaged in any particular job or function. And this observation was reinforced by a general air of idleness, of indifference, even of hopelessness, that seemed to hang about the ship and its crew as a whole.

There was curiously little communication among the crew members Miles watched. They moved about singly, as individuals, and at no time during the three or four hours he watched did he see two of them engage in anything lengthy enough to be called a conversation. On the other hand, there was a curious pattern of behavior that seemed to hold them all. It was a pattern that Miles at first *felt*, with that same new sensitivity to the emotions of others that had been wakened in him by the Center Aliens. He felt it·without being able to trace it to any specific actions or lack of actions. Then, gradually, he began to interpret what he sensed.

Briefly put, it seemed that each individual aboard had certain other individuals whom he ignored. And to all individuals that he did not ignore, he deferred. Furthermore, he in turn was ignored by all the individuals to whom he deferred.

As, Miles suddenly realized, the bearlike alien had ignored him, after one brief glance, when they had met in the corridor earlier.

It dawned on Miles that everyone except Chak'ha had ignored him since he had entered this ship—and in particular had ignored him during his exploratory tour of the vessel just now before coming to the lounge.

With that, the answer came plainly to him. There was evidently a pecking order aboard, a social system in which each member of the crew was deferential to those above him and contemptuous of those beneath. There were no equals on the ship then. Obviously, the way you moved up in rank was to fight your way up—as he had fought and beaten Chak'ha, thereby making Chak'ha last and least. For in such a system a newcomer like Miles himself, entering the ship as someone without his position in the order established, would be challenged first by the lowest member of the pecking order.

So now with his victory over Chak'ha, he was second from the bottom in that order, thought Miles. Why—the remembered, inviting white passion of battle glowed suddenly again to life inside him—all he needed to do to improve his situation on this ship was to fight his way up through the ranks. There could be no danger of losing his life in the process, since evidently the Center Aliens who had built the vessel had made provision against such killing.

Anyone, then, with the guts to take the necessary punishment could challenge anyone else aboard with impunity. Chak'ha, after all, for all his saber teeth, would not have been too difficult to handle if his attack had not come without warning. Obviously, the tigerish alien knew nothing of wrestling, or he would have shown the knowledge during the fighting before Miles had clamped the full nelson on him and caused the fight to be stopped.

None of the other aliens aboard whom Miles had seen—except perhaps the bearlike one—looked like an impossibly powerful or dangerous opponent. Of course, now that Miles had learned that they were not allowed to kill or cripple one another, he could probably not count on another explosion of hysterical strength to help him win, as it had with Chak'ha.

But on the other hand, with a little study of his opponents and a plan of attack—above all, making sure that he was the one who did the attacking, without warning. . . .

An emotional reaction set in suddenly, like a cold and heavy wave of seawater taking him in the face and leaving him gasping. Miles sat stiffly, shocked at his own thoughts.

Could this be he, Miles, sitting here and eagerly measuring the other occupants of the lounge with a careful eye to see how vulnerable they might be to his own teeth, nails, and muscles?

Disgust and anger with himself welled up inside him. So this was all it had been worth, all those years of his painting and theorizing and working? Nothing more than something he could forget in a minute, once he was given a new, strong, two-armed body to play at fighting with, under rules that guaranteed he could not be badly hurt or killed?

What had happened to him?

For that matter, what had happened to the purpose for which he had been brought here? Had he been physically rebuilt, charged with the hopes of a world of people, and shipped out here to the edge of the intergalactic dark just so that he could come to this ship and roll on the deck fighting with equally charged members of other races like his own?

If so, there was something the Center Aliens had not told him—something suspicious and potentially rotten about this whole business of the Silver Horde and the Battle Line.

But whatever it was, beginning now, he was going to make it his business to find it out. Meanwhile, he told himself grimly, he would not be tricked again into losing his emotional perspective.

He would remember that inside this superbly healthy and unkillable body with two strong arms was still the mind and identity of the thin, tense, one-armed human named Miles Vander. Miles Vander, who had a people to

72

save and paintings to paint. He would remember he was not here to fight Chak'has. He was here to fight the Silver Horde, if the Silver Horde honestly existed, not to struggle for some position in a physical pecking order aboard this one small ship.

Perhaps the Center Aliens were not to blame, and it was just that the other racial representatives aboard had not been able to remember that. Perhaps, isolated and waiting here, they had done their best to keep in mind the original purpose that had brought them here and had still failed, giving in at last to the boredom and loneliness of their situation, surrounded by strangers of races other than their own.

He, however, would not be breaking like that. Now that he had been awakened to the danger, he felt the old, inflexible determination that had become part of him back on Earth hardening like spring steel inside him.

He would never break, because he was not like his fellow alien crew members on this ship—not like anyone else in the universe. He was Miles Vander, who had a special personal memory of loneliness and years of striving to make sure he would not give in.

7

The tiger-faced head of Chak'ha rolled upon the bunk—rolled away from the gaze of Miles. Clearly Chak'ha did not want to talk about it.

Miles had come back to the room of the ship in which he had awakened. Chak'ha was still there, lying on his bunk. But when Miles had started to question him about the pecking order, the combats, and the relationship of all this to the coming of the Silver Horde, he had felt unhappiness rising from the lax body of the alien like a cloud of sickness.

"There's just nothing to do," Chak'ha said, looking away from him now, looking at the blank inner wall of his bunk. "There's just nothing else to do."

"Nothing to do but fight with each other?" Miles demanded. "No training to be done? No practicing with our weapons? No practicing with the ship itself? What kind of fighting ship is this?"

"It isn't a fighting ship," said Chak'ha to the wall. "It's the *Fighting Rowboat*."

"The *Fighting Rowboat*?"

"That's what we all call her," muttered Chak'ha.

Miles stared at him. In their common shipboard language, the name Chak'ha had just given the ship was a bitter sneer at the vessel and all those aboard her. The name connoted not only worthlessness, but puffed-up, bragging worthlessness—as if someone whose duty it was to fight should be nicknamed the Ferocious Mouse. Chak'ha remained with his face turned away, offering no further explanation.

"Look at me!" ordered Miles. Slowly, reluctantly, the tiger mask turned back to confront him.

"What do you mean, this isn't a fighting ship?" demanded Miles.

"I mean what I say," said Chak'ha stubbornly. "This ship will never fight anything—let alone the Silver Horde."

"How do you know?"

"Everybody knows," said Chak'ha with a sullen air of hopelessness. "Everybody on the ship knows. We began to know it when we found out they didn't care what happened to us or what we did here."

"Who didn't care? The Center Aliens?" said Miles.

"Them. All the others in this Battle Line," said Chak'ha. "It's plain they don't care. It became plain to the first few of us who arrived here. Wait. You'll see. You'll find out that it makes no difference to them what happens to us—except that we aren't allowed to kill each other when we fight. You saw how you and I were stopped."

"Well, if we aren't here to fight the Silver Horde, what are we here for?" said Miles harshly.

"Who knows?" replied Chak'ha gloomily. "I suppose the Center Aliens know, but they're not likely to tell us."

"Nobody—no one aboard this ship knows?" demanded Miles.

Chak'ha, without moving upon his bunk, gave the impression of shrugging to Miles' emotion-sensitive perceptions.

"Maybe some of the higher-up ones here know," he said. "Maybe Eff"—the name was a sound like the letter *f* prolonged and ending in a sharp whistle—"who's second. Or Luhon, who can beat anybody aboard. Maybe somebody like that knows. I don't."

"Which one's Luhon?" demanded Miles. "I'll ask him."

Chak'ha's head rolled on the bunk, negatively.

"He won't tell you."

"Never mind that," said Miles. "Tell me which one he is."

"He's thin and quick and gray-skinned," said Chak'ha in a lifeless voice, "and his external ears are pointed."

Without a further word, Miles turned and went out of the room. He reentered the lounge and studied its occupants, but none of them fitted the description Chak'ha had given him. He turned and went back through the ship, searching through the other crew quarters—at least those rooms of which the doors were not closed. Still he met nobody fitting the description he had been given. Finally, he turned and went forward. There, alone in the bow control room, he saw a slight, gray-skinned, furless individual with ears that would have fitted well on a pixie or elf out of Earth's legends. Whoever he was, if he was Luhon, he looked like a light-bodied, harmless being to have outfought everybody else aboard the ship. Miles studied him for a second, watching him from the doorway of the control room. The other was playing with the keys on a control console. He ignored Miles, as all aboard had ignored him, and Miles was able to notice how smoothly and swiftly the fingers of the other moved. For all his apparent slightness of limb, he must have muscle if he topped the pecking order, Miles concluded, and if suppleness and his ordinary speed of movement were any index, it might be that his speed was really remarkable. It was hard to believe that this slim creature sitting before him could be at the head of the social system aboard the ship. Still, Miles reminded himself, for all his ferocious appearance, Chak'ha had turned out to be least of them all. Appearances plainly were no index to the dangerousness of his fellow crew members.

Miles went forward into the room until he stood just behind the other individual, who appeared to be checking out the console of the control board before him. Glancing at that control board now, Miles was surprised, for a fleeting second, to discover that he understood its controls as well as he understood the common language they spoke aboard the ship. Then he swung his attention back to his reason for coming here.

"Are you Luhon?" he demanded.

The other neither turned nor moved. Instead, he went on with his movements, ignoring Miles as if Miles were nowhere in existence, let alone less than three feet behind him.

"I said," repeated Miles, slowly and distinctly, "are you Luhon? If you are, I want to talk to you."

The other continued to work with his controls, apparently deaf and blind to the presence of Miles in the same room with him.

"I don't want to fight with you," said Miles evenly, keeping the white flare of his newly discovered battle lust and fury carefully under control. "I only want some information from you—information I think I have a right to have. I only want to know whether it's true that this ship will never go into battle against the Silver Horde and, if that's true, why the Center Aliens brought us all here together after all. If you don't know the answer to either of those things, you don't have to speak. All you have to do is shake your head."

Luhon's head did not move. He went on with what he was doing.

Miles waited as the seconds fled away into minutes.

"Will you answer me?" he said at last, clenching his teeth on the anger building inside of him.

Luhon made no response.

Suddenly the inner fury broke loose in Miles. It boiled up whitely inside him. His arm muscles tensed and jerked with the impulse to reach out, grab the other by the shoulders, spin him around, and choke an answer out of him.

Luhon still continued what he was doing, unperturbed.

But just in time, Miles noticed the pointed right ear twitch and flick backward in Miles' direction.

Caution clamped sudddenly again on Miles. Apparently he was not as ignored as he had thought. Evidently Luhon was not only aware of him, but confident enough of his own physical superiority to stay with his back turned to Miles—practically inviting Miles to attack first. Such confidence, coupled with the fact that Luhon was acknowledged by Chak'ha to be first in the pecking order among the twenty-three members of the crew, rang a sudden warning in Miles.

The time might come, thought Miles, when he might want to have it out with Luhon. But not yet—not, at least, until he had seen more of the other, particularly in action, and discovered the source of Luhon's power and victory over his fellow crew members.

Miles turned and went out of the control room. He went back through the ship, out through the open hatch and down the steps onto the open platform on which the ship lay. He needed to think, and in order to think clearly, he needed to get completely away from the apparent puzzle of the ship, with its twenty-three representatives of twenty-three races apparently brought here for no purpose but to quarrel and to fight with one another.

He explored the platform. It was a flat structure—like a raft in the blackness of the surrounding space, harshly and metallically revealed by the unmoving, unchanging glare of the artificial sun that the Center Aliens had apparently set up to illuminate the Battle Line. From where Miles stood on the platform that artificial sun was larger than, but not as yellow as, the sun of Earth. It had a white, fluorescent glare, which his eyes could not endure to look at directly for more than a fraction of a second. The shadows this light cast on the surface of the raft were as hard and sharp and black as those cast by rocks on an airless moon. Miles walked around the platform and discovered a sort of shed, which he entered. Inside were twenty-three strange machines and stores of what appeared to be—judging by the fact that one of them was a pile of earthly foodstuffs—special rations for each of the various crew members aboard the ship. Miles went on through the shed and out a door at the far end. Behind the shed he saw, lying in a metal cradle, a smaller craft which looked like a miniature version of their ship. It was apparently some sort of courier boat, with two seats inside it.

Inspiration woke in him. He went hastily up to the ship, slid open the door in its side, and climbed in, closing the door behind him. Seating himself in one of the seats, he examined the control board of the small vessel.

As he had suspected, the controls here were immediately as understandable to him as the controls at which Luhon had been working in the larger ship had been. The white anger, still surging below the conscious level in him, erupted suddenly in a flare of new determination.

He would get an answer—one way or another.

He touched the controls of the ship before him with hands as sure as if they had practiced for years. The little ship floated upward from its cradle, turned slowly in the blue-white glare of the artifical sun, and headed up the Battle Line.

For a few seconds it seemed rather to hang in space than to move. But then, without any physical feeling of acceleration, it apparently began to move faster and faster. The nearer ships of the line swelled up on the vision screen before him and fled past it, one by one. There was no sensation of any change in the rate of speed with which it moved, but Miles began to perceive that this small ship went quickly while between the anchored vessels, then slowed down for a few miles on either side of each ship's location while passing, then took up again its between-ship velocity. A feeling of exhilaration began to warm and glow within Miles. At his fingertips, the little ship moved as if it were an extension of his own physical being. He felt as if its speed were his speed; its power, his power; its sureness of response, his own.

Now he was already past the area of smaller, intermediate, and odd-shaped alien ships and approaching the first of the large globe-shaped ships of the Center Aliens. He could see the first of them now, far ahead of him at full magnification on the battle screen built into the console on which his fingers rested—

Without warning, there was someone alongside him in

the other seat of the two-man ship. Miles turned his head and looked.

It was one of the Center Aliens. He was so like the two who had brought Miles from Earth, in the stillness of his pseudohuman features, that for a moment Miles thought one of his old acquaintances had rejoined him. But then he felt the stranger-quality in this particular Center Alien—as he had felt emotional differences in Chak'ha and Luhon and others of his own crew. This Center Alien said nothing; but his hands rested on the other console, which was a duplicate of the control console before Miles, and the little ship turned and headed back the way it had come.

For a second Miles stared. Then his own fingers leaped to the conttrols before him. But there was no response from the ship. It was as if his console had gone dead and only the one in front of the Center Alien controlled the ship.

"What're you doing?" snapped Miles, turning to the other. "I want to talk to somebody—somebody in authority!"

"Talk to me," answered the Center Alien. There was no inflection to his words, but Miles felt an indifference in the alien as remote and icy as contempt. The other continued to drive the two-man vessel back the way it had come, without looking at Miles.

"I was told our ship isn't ever going to fight the Silver Horde!" said Miles. "Is that true?"

"Quite true," answered the Center Alien.

"Then why bring me out here in the first place?" demanded Miles. "Why bring any of us on the *Fighting Rowboat*?"

"It's true that individually, and even collectively, you add little directly to our general Battle Line strength," answered the Center Alien. "All of you together amount to less than one of the least of my own people in that respect. But there is more than the direct addition of strength to be considered. Besides his own personal powers, which vary widely from individual to individual, each one in the Battle Line has a function in which all are equal. That is to act as a resonator, or amplifier, of the

79

group strength and as a channel through which that strength may be directed at the enemy. There is what you might call a feedback effect—from the group to the individual and back again—where the psychic force is concerned."

"Feedback?" Miles stared at him. "Psychic force?"

"The weapons aboard your ship, and aboard all our ships," said the Center Alien, as their small two-man ship continued to slide past the odd-shaped vessels of the Center Aliens' outer allies, "have a dual function. They bring to bear against enemy ships not only a physical, but what I call a *psychic* force. 'Psychic' is not the correct word, but it is the closest I can come to a word in your understanding. The physical element of these weapons is effective enough—it can rip open any Horde ship that comes within effective range. But it is the weapons' ability to project our general psychic strength against the invaders on which our whole strategy of defense is based."

Miles frowned.

"Why?" he asked.

"Because the strategy of the Horde's attack is based, by contrast, on the overwhelming numbers of its ships and people," said the alien. "The Horde counts on being able to pay any price required by a battle, just as long as for every dozen or hundred or thousand of its own ships which are lost, it accomplishes the destruction of at least one opposing ship."

"A thousand for one?" Miles looked narrowly at the other.

"At least that high," replied the Center Alien emotionlessly. "The basic belief of the Horde is that it can afford the losses in ships that any enemy force can inflict on it and still have enough of its own ships left to conquer. But there is, we hope, a point at which even the Horde will refuse to pay the price of conquest. And it is this point we hope to reach with the aid of a psychic force."

Miles frowned again. The words of the Center Alien sounded as if they should make sense to him, but at the same time their real meaning seemed to skitter away from his understanding like a dried leaf before a November wind.

"The psychic force can kill then?" he asked.

"No." The Center Alien spoke the short negative word briefly. "The psychic force is no more than that same strength of identification you absorbed from those individuals of your home world who felt for you before you left. Ask yourself if that feeling inside you can kill. Identification implies empathy, and an emphathic response cannot be used to destroy, being creative in nature. Creation and destruction are antithetical within the same process, just as synthesis and analysis cannot proceed by the same process at the same time—or, in terms possibly more familiar to you, you cannot drive one of your home world's automobiles in forward and reverse gear off the same motor at the same time. Even if it were possible to do this from an engineering standpoint, the two attempts at motion in opposite directions would cancel each other out into motionlessness—a nonexistence of motion. So with any attempt to kill using the psychic force."

"Then I don't follow you," said Miles grimly.

"I am explaining," said the Center Alien, "why our weapons have a physical as well as psychical element. The psychic force cannot kill—but it can control, to the extent of dominating the individual by the group will or the will of the lesser group by the greater. So we will use it against the Horde. With sufficient outflow of psychic power, we hope to hold paralyzed all the invaders who come within range of our weapons while our weapons destroy them."

He paused. Miles nodded slowly.

"I see," said Miles thoughtfully.

"Yes," said the Center Alien, "you see. By this means we hope, not to conquer the Horde—for that is impossible—but to convince them that we can slaughter them almost at will, while remaining very nearly invulnerable to their weapons, and so make them pay such a heavy price in lost ships for each ship of ours they manage to destroy that they will turn away toward some other galaxy that may be less strongly defended against them."

"If the psychic force is that effective," said Miles harshly, "why can't we on the *Fighting Rowboat* be with you when you hit the Horde with your own ships?"

"Because the psychic force is not, in fact, that ef-

81

fective," said the alien. "Each use of it requires an expenditure of energy by each of the individuals making use of it. As long as they do not become weary, these individuals may not only use their own innate psychic force, but also may draw on our general pool of strength and channel it through themselves to make them many times as effective as they would be alone. But the energy of no one, not even us of the Center, is inexhaustible, and you twenty-three would become exhausted very much more quickly than we. Exhausted, an individual loses contact with the general pool of strength. In such a case you would face the Horde with only your own feeble psychic powers and physical weapons, and your ship's destruction by the Horde would follow almost immediately."

"What of it?" demanded Miles. "It's our necks we're risking—"

"They are not yours alone," interrupted the alien. "You refuse to understand. As contributors of original psychic force your twenty-three are nothing—less than the weakest of one of my own race, all of you combined. So that if we lost you, we would lose less than one effective individual unit like myself in terms of original force. But as resonators and amplifiers, you are individually equal to all other individuals in the Battle Line. So that in losing you in that respect, we would be losing the equivalent of twenty-three units."

He paused.

"Do you see now," he said, "why we prefer to keep you back out of the battle and safe, where we can draw on you for resonated strength, without risking your almost certain loss if you joined us in the fighting?"

Again he paused. But Miles said nothing.

"You are unhappy about this," said the Center Alien. "That is because you are still a victim of those primitive emotions which we of the Center long ago amputated from our own egos so that we would continue the intellectual development that has made us what we have become. Because you have such emotions, you assume that we have them also and that our decisions about you are colored by emotion. But they are not. Here in this Battle Line, you are just as a group of chimpanzees would be

82

back on your native world armed with high-powered rifles. The fact that the chimpanzee can be rote-trained to hold the rifle and pull its trigger does not mean it can be trusted with the weapon in the sense that a human soldier could be trusted to carry, maintain, and use his gun effectively against an enemy. That is why, when we actually join battle with the Horde—and whether we do or not will depend on whether our Center computational matrix calculates that we have a chance for victory if we do join battle— the actual fighting contact will be made by us of the Center and some few of the older, more advanced races on whom we can rely. It is simple logic that dictates this, as it dictates that you be held out of the fight and safe."

Miles stared ahead into the vision screen of the small craft. In that screen now, he saw the distant, fast-swelling shape of the platform on which the *Fighting Rowboat* rested.

"The numbers of the Horde," said the Center Alien, "are literally beyond your imagination. Equally beyond you are the questions and factors involved in the function of this Battle Line, which would not exist here and now if it were not for us of the Center. Face the fact that these things are too great for your mind to grapple with, and resign yourself to your situation."

They were almost on the platform now. The Center Alien said no more but brought the little ship in for a landing in its cradle. As it touched down, he disappeared from the seat beside Miles. Wrapped in his own bitter thoughts, Miles slowly opened the door on his side of the craft and climbed out. He went back into the main ship.

But this time he avoided both the control room and the lounge. Instead, he went down the connecting corridors until he came to the first of the weapons, standing isolated and alone within its empty transparent bubble that faced outward into the blackness of intergalactic space. For a long moment he stood looking at it, and now his mind, alerted by what the Center Alien had said, saw with the same sort of knowledge that had told him about the control consoles of both ships that these weapons had been neglected and ignored.

It was not that they were rusted or decayed. There was

no sign of dust or cobwebs on them. But with that feeling part of his mind which had become so sensitive lately, Miles felt the coldness of long disuse that hung like a fog about the weapon before him. Feeling it now, he began to understand at least part of what the Center Alien had been trying to tell him. Psychic force must pulse through this device before him if it were to help destroy the Horde. But he also now recognized something that the Center Alien had not bothered to tell him. If this weapon were to be operated in battle, a certain amount of the psychic force of whatever individual operated it would necessarily have to be used up first merely to warm it up in a psychic sense, before it would fire. *That* was the penalty of the long disuse with which the twenty-three aboard this ship had treated it. It confirmed the indifference, amounting to contempt, of the Center Alien as he had explained his superiority over Miles on the way back here.

It did more. It explained the self-contempt in which the twenty-three held themselves. Their undeniable, unavoidable knowledge of their own inferiority and uselessness compared to the power and wisdom of the Center Aliens—in fact, to everyone else in this Battle Line. It would be that knowledge and self-contempt which had driven them to set up the pecking order, so that all but the weakest of them would have at least one other individual to whom they could feel superior.

Miles became aware that his jaw muscles were aching. He had clenched them some time since. He forced himself to relax them. Inside him, his understanding of the situation here was complete at last, carved on his mind like letters in stone.

What use was it to them—to himself and the human race—to be physically saved from extermination if the price of that saving was to face the fact that their greatest accomplishments and dreams were less than line drawings on a cave wall and that in the eyes of the race which dominated the galaxy, men were no more than ape-men scratching themselves mindlessly as they lolled in the sun?

The Center Alien had advised him to resign himself to the situation. Miles laughed harshly. Wise and powerful the Center Aliens might be, but here was proof that their wisdom and knowledge were not all-perfect.

If nothing else, they had underestimated humans—and Miles himself. Powered by that same capacity for emotion that this advanced people had despised and discarded, Miles knew that he was no more capable of resignation than an eagle is of forgetting he has wings. There was no point in his trying resignation.

Therefore, he would not. The old, familiar, grim determination that had kept him at his painting formed within him again now, but with a new purpose. Deeply, he realized now that he was not afraid of the Silver Horde or daunted by the Center Aliens. He was not about to obey the latter blindly, as if they were but one more superior member of a larger pecking order.

He would make up his own mind about what he would do. And that meant that in spite of both Horde and Center Aliens, the *Fighting Rowboat* would take its place in the battle—when the time came. Yes, the *Fighting Rowboat* would fight—if he had to take her out alone against the Silver Horde, she would fight.

8

"Tell me his name again," said Miles.

"His name is Vouhroi," replied Chak'ha.

They were seated together in the ship's lounge. Miles had made Chak'ha bring his own chair and table unit over close beside Miles' own. Now, unlike all the others aboard the ship, they sat in the lounge together in conversation, as they had for nearly two weeks now. Chak'ha had resisted this closeness at first, but Miles had forced it. Then, in the end, the tiger-faced alien had yielded and accepted what was almost a friendship. In fact, he had become more dependent on it than was Miles, so that he followed Miles about and stayed close to him as many of their waking hours as was possible.

No doubt the other twenty-one aboard the ship had observed this conversational closeness. But since Miles and Chak'ha were together at the bottom of the pecking order, it seemed that none of the others would lower themselves to notice their exception to the normal social pattern aboard the vessel. So for nearly two weeks, undisturbed, Miles had been able to study the others as they moved about the ship and occasionally—without apparent reason—merged in battle or continued to ignore or give way to one another in accordance to their relative positions in the pecking order.

Luhon was the leader—there was no doubt about that. Just below him was Eff, who, oddly enough, turned out to be the rotund, bearlike alien who had seemed so harmless to Miles at first sight. These two seemed satisfied with their relative positions. But below the rank of Eff the mambers of the pecking order were continually being challenged by the members immediately below them.

"Why do they keep fighting, when the same one always loses and the same one always wins?" Miles had asked Chak'ha.

Chak'ha shook his head.

"I don't know, but," he said, "I think it's because we've got nothing else to do. Fighting is all we've got. And the fight just might turn out differently the next time."

Miles had nodded. He had carefully set himself to learn the rank of each crew member in the pecking order, but his interest had centered on Vouhroi, who was next above Miles himself now that Miles had conquered Chak'ha.

Miles had begun to plan. He could do nothing until he was in control of the others aboard this ship. That meant winning his way to the top of the pecking order. Vouhroi was the first step he must mount. He had studied Vouhroi, therefore, not merely with the desire of someone wanting to improve his rank among his fellows for his own satisfaction, but with the same combination of hunger, fury, and creative desire with which he had attacked his paintings, back on Earth. It was a method of attack that would not consider any result short of success.

Physically, Miles told himself, each of the others aboard must have some point or points at which he was vulnerable. Weak spots. What were the weak spots of Vouhroi?

The one he studied was a lean but powerful-looking, catlike alien. Not heavily catlike as was the tigerish

86

Chak'ha, but with the long-legged, high-haunched feline grace of a Canadian lynx. Vouhroi's chair in the lounge was almost directly opposite that of Miles, and while he had never overtly acknowledged Miles' existence, Miles had come to be expert at reading the small signs in the other aliens that warned him that they were aware of his presence and braced against any sudden unexpected attack by him.

Clearly, of all the others, Vouhroi, who was next in line above Miles, was not about to be taken by surprise by any unexpected attack by Miles. His back was always to the wall, and his eyes—though apparently focused generally on the room—always included Miles within their range of vision. Though apparently relaxed, when Miles was present the lynxlike alien was always in a position from which he could get to his feet in an instant.

Nor was this treatment just for Miles. Everyone in the pecking order, Miles noticed, watched the individual just below him in the same way.

A surprise attack, the jumping of your opponent from behind or in a second of disadvantage, was only one more tactic in the ruleless battles that were fought between members of the crew. No advantage was unfair if it led to winning. Cold-bloodedly Miles made plans to make use of the unfair advantages at his disposal. He gave Chak'ha instructions.

The end result of those instructions was the conversation that they were having now as they sat in the lounge looking across at Vouhroi. The timbre of Miles' voice and that of Chak'ha's were very close—close enough so that practice could make them almost identical. For more than a week now, Miles had been secretly practicing with Chak'ha to imitate the pronunciation Chak'ha gave to Vouhroi's name.

Now he repeated the name after Chak'ha. The tiger-faced alien nodded.

"Right," he said at last. "It sounds right the way you say it now."

"Good," answered Miles. He glanced across at Vouhroi, apparently dozing, with half-closed eyelids, across the lounge. "I'll go forward now. You wait a few minutes and then stroll aft."

Miles got up from his chair in the lounge and wandered toward the front end of the lounge and from there into the corridor leading to the control room in front. He went halfway up the corridor, turned, put his shoulders against the wall, and waited.

With his mind he measured the slow seconds as they flowed by. Ever since the Center Aliens had changed him physically, he had been aware of differences in mind and mental skills as well. One of these was this ability to keep time in his head as well as any watch. So he waited while the minutes passed, and after perhaps three and a half minutes Eff came down the corridor from the control room, gave him the barest glance, and passed on without pausing, his rotund figure disappearing into the lounge. Miles waited another minute and a half. Then, quietly, he walked down the corridor until he was just out of sight of the lounge and the position of Vouhroi's chair in the lounge.

From where he stood flattened against the inside wall of the corridor, he could just see the entrance to the farther corridor leading back to the crew quarters and could see against the inner wall there the blocky outline of Chak'ha, waiting.

Then he shouted, in the closest imitation of Chak'ha's voice and accent he could manage.

"Vouhroi!"

"Vouhroi!" It was a shout in Chak'ha's voice from the other corridor. Chak'ha was now running into the lounge, continuing to shout as he came. "Vouhroi! Vouhroi! Vouhroi . . ."

Miles launched himself toward the lounge, running at top speed and as noiselessly as he could. He had a moment's glimpse of Chak'ha rushing in from the opposite direction—of Vouhroi with his back turned, staring at Chak'ha. Then Miles hit the lynxlike alien with a hard tackle at waist level.

He slammed the unprepared Vouhroi down against the deck of the lounge—hard enough, Miles would have thought, to knock out a human being. But even as he was thrown to the deck, Vouhroi was attempting to twist around in Miles' grasp, and though his head slammed hard on the uncarpeted surface beneath them, he did not appear to be stunned.

Miles already had Vouhroi in the same full nelson which had worked so well with Chak'ha. At the same time that Miles began to exert pressure against the other's neck, he clamped his own human legs around the legs of Vouhroi and tried to hold them as Vouhroi attempted to kick and scramble loose. But the alien's legs were too powerful. They broke free, and Miles shifted his leg grip to a scissors hold around Vouhroi's narrow waist.

Vouhroi surged about and for one furious moment succeeded in rising to his feet, with Miles riding on his back. Then Miles' weight overbalanced him and he fell backward. Lying underneath the alien, Miles continued to apply pressure to Vouhroi's neck. He half expected the overdrive strength to come to his aid, as it had with Chak'ha. But it did not come, and it was not needed.

Already Vouhroi's neck was starting to give. It did not, indeed, have as much inner stiffness and strength as had Chak'ha's. Miles felt it bend—and almost at once the tranquilizing gray fog, the feeling of weakness and indifference, closed in about him and his opponent, and he drifted dimly off into unconcern, the battle fires of emotion within him damped and extinguished.

When he woke on his bunk after this second battle, however, there was a face looming close above him. It was the face of Chak'ha, and coming from Chak'ha, Miles sensed clearly a strange emotion—something between glee and triumph.

"Awake, Miles?" asked Chak'ha.

"Awake," replied Miles a little thickly.

The face of Chak'ha came closer. He lowered his voice to what, for him, was the equivalent of a whisper.

"We did it, Miles! Didn't we do it?"

"I did it," said Miles. "With your help."

"That's what I mean," whispered Chak'ha savagely. "With my help. You did it with *my* help. The two of us together."

Chak'ha's eyes half-closed. Once more there came from him, to Miles' emotion-sensing capability, a feeling of great relief and joy and friendship.

For the first time, Miles realized that Chak'ha had expected to be disowned by Miles once Miles had moved one more step up the ladder. There was something deeply touching about the emotion that flowed from the tiger-faced individual bent closely above his bunk. Miles reached out to grasp one of the thick, stubby, clawed hands of Chak'ha in his own. Chak'ha looked down at the joined extremities in surprise.

"This is how we do it among my people," said Miles and shook Chak'ha's hand, then let it go. Chak'ha looked for a moment wonderingly at his own released hand, then stared back at Miles, and the feeling of happiness from him increased.

Miles drifted back off into slumber, carrying that feeling of happiness and friendship with him.

In the next few weeks that followed, he fought his way up through the pecking order. In each case, after winning, he tried to make friends with the alien he had just conquered. One or two of those he had beaten became friendly. But none of them became as close to him as Chak'ha, who now followed him about continually. In time, there were left only two crew members aboard who did not acknowledge Miles' presence or answer when he spoke to them. These were Eff and Luhon, the one whom nobody else could beat.

The opposition had grown progressively more difficult as Miles had mounted the ladder of the pecking order. His last fight, with a dark-skinned humanoid named Henaoa, had taken all of Miles' strength and skill to win. Logically, therefore, he could not expect to conquer the two remaining crew members. Even if he did somehow manage to conquer Eff, certainly he would not be able to conquer Luhon.

The secrets of their individual strengths were now quite clear to him. In Eff's case, the rotund body was all muscle—he was not plump; he was a chunk of heavy-bodied power. In Luhon's case, his secret was that speed which Miles had already observed. Certainly there must be strength connected with it. But in any case, Luhon's reflexes were such that it would be necessary for Miles to conquer the gray-skinned alien with his first blow—because the chances were that he would not have a chance to land a second.

But Luhon was in the future. Eff was in the present, and Miles was aware that Eff had been subtly on guard ever since Miles' last victory—for all that the rotund alien appeared to ignore everyone but Luhon.

For a full week, Miles studied Eff. At first it seemed that there was no point of weakness about him. The joints of his body were solid and deeply set in muscle and flesh. His neck was so short as to be almost nonexistent. The full nelson that Miles had used to advantage several times now would not work this time—let alone the fact that Eff had undoubtedly noted its use and was on guard. Miles raked over the dead coals of his younger memories before polio had stricken and made useless his arm. There must have been other wrestling holds or tricks that he must have known or read about or heard about, once upon a time. He needed something unexpected to use against Eff.

In the end, he concentrated his study on Eff's waist and the lower part of his trunk. As far as he could discover, the bearlike alien had a humanlike chest, ribs, and diaphragm. There was just a chance in that fact, if Miles could catch Eff at the right spot in the ship.

He had to wait several days before that chance came. During those days he stayed close to Eff, who only by the merest flicker of an eyelid or twitch of a furry ear acknowledged the fact he was being followed. But Eff's vigilance did not relax. In spite of this, the time came when Miles, following closely behind him, saw Eff less than two arm's lengths away from him, turning from the corridor around a little angle into the lounge.

Miles leaped upon him from behind.

Eff had been on guard against any attack, and he was turning to face Miles even as Miles hit him. But Miles had waited for just this place to start the fight. The momentum of his charge drove the bearlike alien into the angle where two walls met, so that in falling, Eff was crowded into the corner. He went down on his side, with Miles' legs closing about the thick waist and one furry arm. As they landed on the floor, Miles caught Eff's remaining free arm in both hands and twisted it up behind the stocky body.

Even with his two arms against Eff's one, he found it almost impossible to keep that other arm imprisoned. The arm caught by Miles' legs, however, was held. Eff's shoulder was wedged in the corner, his arm and waist imprisoned by the muscles of Miles' interlocked legs in a scissors grip which Miles proceeded now to tighten around Eff's waist, his left knee driving hard up into the alien's diaphragm area just below the rib cage.

Eff struggled—but they were locked together. Miles could do no more than hold Eff's left arm twisted up behind him while their combined weights and the scissors hold kept the other arm pinned. To the watching crew members that soon gathered in a semicircle around them, it seemed as if nothing were happening. But a great deal was happening of which only Eff and Miles were conscious.

But Miles' left knee was continuing a steady pressure, pushing, grinding in and up against the bottom of Eff's lungs, driving the air out of them.

They lay there together in the angle of the wall, seeming barely to move. But the struggle continued—for an intolerably long time, it seemed to Miles. He could feel that the pressure of his legs was gradually shortening the breath available to Eff, but Eff did not seem weakened. Every so often he surged mightily, if without success, against the hold with which Miles was keeping him pinned.

But now Miles felt his own strength leaking away. He had only so much muscle power in his arms and legs, and that power was gradually being exhausted in keeping the heavier and stronger alien beneath him tied up. He felt himself beginning to weaken—and overdrive was not coming to his aid. He almost gave up—and then the old, familiar determination rose in him. Through the bones of his head, he heard his teeth grinding together. He would crush this enemy of his. Crush . . . crush. . . .

But suddenly the gray, tranquilizing mist was rising about him. He felt his grip slackening, he felt his combat fury ebbing away from him. For a second he was dumb-founded, disbelieving. He had not yet lost. Why was the invisible protective device of the ship stopping the battle? It was not fair. . . .

The gray mist rose inexorably around him.

9

For one wild moment he tried to fight mist and Eff at once.

Then, with the last flicker of conscious thought left to him before the tranquilizing effect stole all feeling from him, understanding woke in him. He realized suddenly that it must be the other way around—that he must have brought Eff to the point of suffocation and un-consciousness, where the tranquilizing effect needed to ex-ert itself to save the rotund alien's life. Miles had won.

This time the tranquilizing effect lifted swiftly. It pulled away from both him and his opponent while they were still lying on the floor of the lounge. Miles pushed away the hands that were trying to lift him and got to his feet unaided. Opposite him, he saw Eff also getting to his feet. The bearlike alien's face opened in a grimace that would never have been recognizable as a smile if the outwash of emotion from the other had not confirmed that a smile was intended. The furry chest was heaving for air, and Eff's words came out in short gasps; but there was a cheerfulness to them that Miles had not yet encountered in any of the aliens aboard whom he had conquered.

"Better . . . than I am," panted Eff. "Now what? I've been wanting to know what you've been after . . . ever since you started fighting your way up to my position on the ship."

Still gasping for air himself, Miles stared at Eff. With the exception of Chak'ha, he had found no crew member desirous or capable enough of friendship to meet him on a level basis after he had conquered him. Invariably the other had assumed the subordinate position.

But apparently, with Eff, being conquered physically did not mean that his soul had been dominated. This was

93

a good sign for the success of the plan in the back of Miles' mind.

"I'll tell you what I'm after," Miles replied, "after I've beaten Luhon."

Around them the other crew members who had been spectators were drifting off. Only Chak'ha remained. Eff glanced at the tiger-faced alien for a second, then back at Miles.

"You'll never beat Luhon," Eff said.

"Yes, I will," said Miles. "I have to. So I'll manage it somehow."

Eff shook his head again, if amiably. His breathing was slowing to a normal rate.

"You'll never beat Luhon," he repeated, not didactically or stubbornly, but in the calm tone of somebody who patiently states a fact to a child or someone of simple intelligence.

"Believe what you like," said Miles. He hesitated, then took a long chance—a chance he had taken with no one so far except Chak'ha. "How about helping me?"

Eff looked him frankly in the face.

"I won't help you fight him," answered Eff. "But outside of that, I'll help you with anything reasonable."

"That's all I ask," said Miles.

Eff grinned more widely. Chak'ha moved in until he stood close to both of them, and the aura of emotion that Miles sensed around all three of them seemed to flow together into one unit of mutual understanding.

From that point on began Miles' first days of anything like comradeship aboard the small vessel.

At first Miles had half expected Chak'ha to resent the sudden inclusion of Eff into what had been a two-way partnership. But he had forgotten that Eff had been high in the pecking order, while Chak'ha had been at the bottom. Chak'ha made no attempt to compete with Eff for Miles' friendship. In fact, as Miles discovered, it would have been hard for anyone to resent Eff.

Once he had opened up to the two of them, the bearlike alien turned out to own a warmth of character closer to human warmth than Miles had found otherwise aboard the ship. Eff was an extrovert. He was frank and—except

94

for his belief that Luhon was unconquerable—apparently daunted by nothing, even including the Center Aliens. Amused by Miles' determination to attempt the apparently hopeless task of fighting Luhon but fascinated by it, he joined happily in helping Miles study Luhon.

"I tell you," Miles kept insisting to him stubbornly, "Luhon has to have a weak spot! Any organism, by its very nature, has to have drawbacks as well as advantages."

"To be sure, he has to have weak spots," replied Eff shrewdly. "But are they weak spots that you have strong spots to correspond with? Luhon's simply too fast for you. He's too fast for any of us aboard here. He's from a heavy world—one where the gravity is much more than any of us is used to."

Miles stared at him.

"You mean," said Miles at last, "he's stronger than he looks, because of that—"

"Stronger? Some, of course." Eff shrugged good-humoredly. "But that's not the point. He's much faster, because of the gravity conditions he's grown up with."

"Faster?" echoed Miles.

Eff laughed.

"You don't understand, Miles?" said the stocky alien. "Stop and think then. The stronger the gravity, the faster an object falls, say from your hand to the ground. Correct?"

"Yes," said Miles slowly.

"Also, the faster *you* fall to the ground, if you get off-balance," said Eff. "Correct?"

"Ah," said Miles, suddenly understanding.

"I see you follow me now," said Eff. "Standing, walking, running—almost everything we bipeds do requires maintaining our balance. And the quicker we fall when our balance is lost, the faster our reflexes have to be to take muscular action to stop us from falling. Luhon is like that—his reflexes are simply that much faster than mine . . . or yours. So I tell you—there's no hope. You will never beat him!"

Miles shook his head. He did not believe that some key could not be found to defeat the slender, quick-moving, gray-skinned alien who continued—out of all those aboard the *Fighting Rowboat*—to ignore him.

In fact, Luhon was isolated now in the old pattern of behavior, for all the rest aboard had begun to associate with and talk to one another, regardless of rank. They did it seldom, and they did it warily, but they were doing it. Miles' friendship with Chak'ha had first broken the ice of the pecking order. Now, slowly but undeniably, a general thaw was setting in.

The exception was Luhon. But if it bothered him to be set aside, separate within the old pattern of behavior aboard the ship, he did not show it. He spent his waking hours working with the ship's controls, and he continued to ignore everyone aboard, Miles included. Nor could Miles notice any increase in the minimal signs that betrayed Luhon's awareness of Miles whenever Miles got within jumping distance of the gray-skinned alien. Moreover, at the end of two weeks of study, with all the help that Eff and Chak'ha could give him, Miles had yet to find any sure counter for that inhuman swiftness of physical reflex Luhon possessed.

The best Miles could do was to plan an attack that would at least give him the advantage of choosing the time and place of battle. He could hope to get in one quick blow—and that would be all. It would need to be a crippling or knockout blow if Miles were to win at all. The best place for it to be landed, Miles thought, was the narrow and apparently soft midsection of Luhon, just above the waist. He planned his blow and rehearsed it in the privacy of the cabin he shared with Chak'ha until it was reflexive, until it was essentially automatic.

Then he stationed himself one day just within the open doorway of his cabin. Eff and Chak'ha took up their posts in the lounge.

Miles waited. It was a long wait, and he ended up sitting rather than standing, until a preliminary signal, which was Chak'ha's own peculiar bark of laughter, alerted him to the fact that Luhon had commenced to move through the lounge headed aft. Miles got swiftly to his feet.

He stepped noiselessly to within half a step of the open doorway and listened, with ears tuned to unnatural acuteness by the tension within him. He heard the footsteps of Luhon approaching down the corridor outside the cabin. A coldness enfolded his forehead, and he knew that he had begun to sweat with anticipation. His heart beat faster. He tensed, poised—

The laugh of Chak'ha rang out again from the lounge.

Miles launched himself forward. He had a glimpse of a gray body before him, swiftly twisting away. His fist grazed a gray side. He felt the shock of a sudden heavy blow at the side of his neck. He caught himself, bounced off a corridor wall, and before he could even try to strike again, another blow somewhere on his head sent him sliding down and away unto unconsciousness. . . .

When he opened his eyes, he found he was lying on his bunk. His neck ached with an ache that seemed to penetrate across his chest and down the opposite side of his body. The faces of Eff and Chak'ha floated above him. He opened his mouth to speak, but to his surprise what came out was barely more than a whisper—and even that hurt his neck.

"What happened?" he whispered.

"What I told you would happen," replied the voice of Eff. "He was too fast for you."

The feeling of disillusionment and defeat closed around Miles like quicksand. He slipped back into unconsciousness.

But when he opened his eyes next, it was from sleep, and it was as if his mind had come to its own conclusion and made itself up while he slumbered. Chak'ha was not in the room, but Eff was. Miles struggled to sit up on the edge of the bed. His neck ached, and his head was dizzy. But he made it. Eff looked at him with a tolerant humor.

"Help me up," husked Miles, even those few words sending pain up through his neck and into his head where it spread into a skullcap of headache.

Eff came forward and pulled Miles to his feet.

"There," said Eff. "Now you're up. But what's the use in that? You're just going to have to lie down again."

"No," whispered Miles. In him was something cold and hard as a nugget of meteoric iron flung through light-years of empty space to its destination, death at last in the fires of a sun. "Help me . . . walk."

He headed toward the doorway of the room, with Eff holding one arm and guiding him. As he went, he seemed to draw strength from the very movement. He turned left down the corridor.

"Where's Luhon?" he whispered hoarsely to Eff.

"Where he almost always is," replied Eff, watching him curiously. "Up front by himself, in the control room."

"Good," husked Miles. He continued to totter on down the corridor, with Eff helping to balance him. But his strength was coming back rapidly with that near-magic return of health that was part of the Center Alien science built into the ship. By the time he was halfway across the lounge he was able to shake himself free of Eff's sustaining grip and walk alone.

When he entered the forward corridor leading to the control room, he was striding a little in advance of Eff. The pain was still in his neck and head, but he could bear it. And the action of his muscles was coming more easily to him—which was important.

Eff caught up with him.

"What're you going to do?" asked Eff.

"Wait and see," answered Miles.

He went on, Eff beside him, until he reached the entrance to the control room. There, as usual, sat Luhon at the controls. But for once his fingers were not playing with them. Instead, his gaze was lifted above them to the control room's main vision screen, which was set now on a view of intergalactic space—looking in that direction from which Miles' implanted inner knowledge told him the Silver Horde was expected to come.

There was something lonely about the way the still, slim, gray-skinned figure sat, with its gaze fixed unmovingly on empty intergalactic space. But Miles had no time for empathy now.

Putting out a hand to stop Eff from following him beyond the open doorway, he walked forward without pausing and, when he was within range, launched himself without any attempt at trickery at the back of Luhon's neck.

This time, when he awoke, he remembered nothing

beyond that single jump forward. His neck, surprisingly, was not so painful now. But his head was one single, solid ache, as if Luhon's retaliation this time had been all in that area. He lay awhile, waiting and hoping for the ache to diminish. But if it did so, it did so only slightly.

He turned his head and saw Chak'ha and Eff watching him. Painfully, once more he struggled to sit up on the edge of the bed. Neither of the others came forward to help him.

Rage suddenly flooded through him—not rage at Luhon, but rage at the two who stood watching.

"Come here!" he croaked hoarsely. "Help me!"

It was not a request he was making of them. It was an order. And there was enough of the old pecking order pattern left in them that both came to him and helped him to his feet. For a moment his head reeled, and the room seemed to spin and sway around him. Then his gaze and sense of balance settled.

He turned toward the doorway of the room.

"To Luhon," he said hoarsely. There was a moment's hesitation on the part of the other two aliens. Then, silently, they each took an elbow and guided him out into the corridor and once more toward the front of the vessel.

This time, as he walked through the lounge—which now was filled with silent, watching crewmen in all their various alien shapes and expressions of feature—recovery was slow in coming to him. But come it did. By the time he was halfway down the corridor toward the control room he was once more walking without assistance.

He made it to the entrance of the control room and there paused. Because this time, evidently alerted by the sound of footsteps approaching, Luhon had turned about in his chair and was facing the doorway. His eyes met the eyes of Miles plainly this time, and for the first time without any pretense of avoidance.

Luhon's face, insofar as six weeks had taught Miles to interpret the gray-skinned alien's features, wore a look of puzzlement. He stared searchingly at Miles in the doorway.

Miles launched himself forward in a tottering rush, his hands outstretched to grab the throat of the other.

But before his hands closed around the gray throat, Luhon was no longer before him. Miles found himself seized and swung about. He was pinned, with his back against the slanting face of one of the control consoles. With ease, Luhon held him helpless there, and the gray-skinned face looked down into Miles' from a distance of a few inches.

"What do you want?" asked Luhon.

It was the first time that Miles had heard the voice of the other. It was a soft, low-pitched voice, a strange voice to belong to someone who had outfought everyone else aboard this vessel. And it, together with the emotions that Miles felt emanating from Luhon, was deep-stained with puzzlement.

"I want"—Miles' voice was almost too husky to be understandable—"to fight the Silver Horde."

For a long moment Luhon's gray features continued to look down into Miles' face. Then Miles felt the grip that was holding him pinioned against the console released. Luhon stood back from him, a slight, slim figure—not only in contrast with Miles, but also with Eff and Chak'ha, who now filled the control room doorway behind the ship's champion.

"You want to fight the Silver Horde?" echoed Luhon in his soft voice. His eyes traveled up and down Miles. "So do I. But, a great deal better than you, I know how impossible a hope that is."

10

Miles slowly straightened up. He rubbed his aching head with a forefinger and tried to clear the hoarse vocal cords of his painful throat.

"You're wrong," he answered Luhon.

"No," said Luhon evenly.

"Yes," said Miles. His weary legs began to tremble, and he sat down in the control seat Luhon had just vacated. "Do you know what I did the first day I was here? I looked around the ship, and then I looked around the platform. And then I took that small courier ship from its cradle on the platform and went in it up the line toward the big ships where the Center Aliens are."

Luhon's pointed ears suddenly pricked and turned forward toward Miles.

"You went in and saw the Center Aliens?" he asked.

"I didn't get as far as I'd planned to go," said Miles. "All of a sudden I found one of them sitting beside me, and he turned the ship around and brought it back. But he answered my questions. He told me why this ship is never intended to fight the Silver Horde. He told me he only wants us for feedback purposes on the total weapons of the total battle line, if it comes to fighting. He told me that one of them is worth more than all twenty-three of us in this ship put together."

Miles stopped talking. Luhon stared at him for a long moment.

"You took that little boat," said Luhon, almost wonderingly. "And you went in—you tried to get in up to where the Center Aliens are. You did that?"

"None of you ever did anything like that, is that it?" he demanded suddenly of Luhon.

Luhon made the negative gesture of his race. It was only a slight twisting of his upper body, but the aura of emotion around him carried the meaning behind it clearly to Miles' emotional sensitivity.

"But you asked him," said Luhon, staring brilliantly at Miles. "And he gave you the answers."

"Yes," said Miles. He struggled to his feet. "Only, I don't believe him. I don't agree with him. I think we *can* fight the Silver Horde—in this ship, the twenty-three of us, working her alongside all the other ships that go out to fight the Horde when the time comes."

Once more Luhon looked at him for what seemed a long time. Then he made a negative twist of his body again; only this time there was something like a shrug in it.

"So you believe that?" demanded the gray-skinned alien. "And that's why you fought your way up to just below me? You wanted to take over this ship to make it into something that could fight the Silver Horde?"

"That's right," said Miles. He added, brutally. "None of

101

the rest of you seemed to have the guts for it."

He tensed, bracing himself for a sudden attack by Luhon.

But the gray-skinned alien only stared at him for a moment longer, then turned half around so that he had both Eff and Chak'ha in the doorway within his field of vision as well as Miles. Then he took a step backward.

"I didn't believe we could fight the Silver Horde," he said. His eyes fastened brilliantly on Miles. "I still don't.' Also, I know that you could never beat me, no matter how many times you try. Do you understand that?"

Miles shook his head.

"No," he said. "You can't kill me. So in the end I'll beat you. No matter how long it takes or how many times I have to try."

Once more, Luhon made that body-twisting movement of negation. But this time it was nearly all shrug.

"You can't beat me, but you'll keep on trying," he said, almost to himself. "You'll keep attacking me until you win, you say. And we all know you can't make this ship into a fighting vessel which the Center Aliens will let go against the Silver Horde when it comes. But you say you'll keep trying until you do."

He took another step back. He looked at Miles, and once more Miles braced himself for a lightning attack. But no attack came.

"All right, then, in that case," said Luhon, "I am defeated."

Miles stared at him. It seemed too sudden, too easy a victory. What had been, dimly but certainly, in the back of his mind was that he would keep on attacking Luhon until he exhausted the other. He had hoped only to be able to bother the gray-skinned alien until Luhon would buy peace at the price of stepping down from the number one position. This sudden admission of defeat made Miles cautious.

"Just like that?" he said, narrowly watching Luhon. "Why?"

"Because," answered Luhon softly, "*I* did not take the little boat and try to talk to the Center Aliens. Because *I* did not plan to fight my way up to the top in this ship for any purpose other than to be on top. Because *I*, even now, don't believe you can make this ship into something that will go out to fight the Silver Horde. But most of all, because I want to fight the Silver Horde as much as you do."

He turned his brilliant gaze toward Eff and Chak'ha.

"All of us aboard here," he said slowly, "have dreamed about fighting when the time comes. Isn't that so, friends?"

For a moment, Eff and Chak'ha stared back at Luhon as if in astonishment at finding themselves directly addressed by him. Then together they made the individual body movements that were the equivalent of a human nod.

"Yes," said Eff. The rough frankness of his usual voice was slowed and more solemn now. "For me—yes. And Chak'ha, here, says yes. If we four feel that way, I'd think the others would feel that way, too."

"They will, I think," said Luhon. "We're a great deal alike, all of us on this ship—more alike than we like to think, considering the differences of body and mind among us. But at least we're alike in being different from those Center Aliens. They don't have feelings, as we do." He turned to Miles. "Isn't that true, friend Miles?"

"They don't feel the way we do, that's certain," said Miles grimly.

"Then it's settled," said Luhon. "I abdicate in favor of you, Miles. For the rest, I think they'll all be glad to join us. If not"—he did not smile (perhaps he could not with the muscles in his gray face), but a touch of humor sped from him like a ripple over the surface of a pond to break against Miles' emotional perceptions—"we'll make them. If there's anything I can do to make it more sure that my people at home survive the Horde, I won't stop at knocking a few heads together here."

"I don't believe it'll be necessary," said Miles. "But let's see."

It was just beginning to sink into him now that Luhon had actually given way, had stepped down and allowed him, Miles, to take top position aboard the *Fighting Rowboat*. The reaction had begun a warm glow that seemed to spread out from the center of his body, soothing all his hurts and aches and clearing his head amazingly. "Let's get them all together in the lounge now and talk to them."

"Yes," said Luhon, "let's go to the lounge."

They went. As they entered the lounge, with Eff and Chak'ha abreast, followed by Luhon beside Miles, and moved to stand together in one corner from which they could survey the rest of the room, the eyes of everyone else there turned to them.

"Get everyone here," said Luhon, raking the room with his eyes. His gaze fastened on Vouhroi, who was closest to the corridor leading back to the crew quarters. "You, Vouhroi, go back and bring everybody else up here."

Vouhroi went. The silence in the lounge continued unbroken. The eyes of those there remained fixed on the four standing in the corner. For the first time a small doubt crawled through the lower level of Miles' mind. They were four combined now—three who were the top three in physical abilities aboard the ship plus Chak'ha, who was least. But with the breakdown of the old pecking order anything was possible. What if, seeing this combination of four, the others of the nineteen remaining moved to combine themselves in an opposing group? Suddenly, he was glad of Luhon's willingness to fight for their plans if necessary.

Five other crew members, followed by Vouhroi, filed into the lounge and filled up the empty chairs, with the exception of those chairs belonging to Miles and his three companions. They sat still, looking at Luhon.

"Miles just conquered me," said Luhon. "So he's on top now aboard this ship. He believes, and we with him here agree, that from now on things are going to be different." He glanced aside at Miles. "Tell them, Miles."

"There isn't going to be any more fighting among ourselves," said Miles, looking around at the different alien faces. "From now on we're going to work together, and we're going to make the *Fighting Rowboat* into a ship that can actually go into battle against the Silver Horde when it comes."

A small sound came murmuring from the rest of the crew members, like the sound of wind through the swaying branches of a grove of trees. It was a combination of sounds, in many verbal ways, of astonishment and disbelief.

"I know!" said Miles swiftly. "The Center Aliens don't think we can do it. But I think we can. Have any of you gotten close to those weapons and felt what they're like with the sensing part of your minds? They're *cold*! We'd have to work with them to warm them up. But who knows what they'd be like if they *were* warmed up?"

He looked around at them.

"We come from fighting races, all of us," he said. "Otherwise we wouldn't have fought among ourselves the way we did. Now, who among you doesn't want to fight the Silver Horde if you get the chance?"

All through the lounge there was silence. No one moved; no one replied.

"None of you!" said Miles. "Of course, if that's the case, what've you got to lose by going along with me? Let's see if this ship and all of us, working together, can't make a fighting unit that the Center Aliens will let join them when the time comes to face the Silver Horde."

He paused. They still looked at him, neither assenting nor dissenting.

"All right," said Miles slowly. "Is there anyone here who won't go along with the rest of us in doing this?"

Beside and behind Miles, Luhon, with Eff and Chak'ha, moved forward a step.

No one spoke. For a moment Miles was tempted to let it go at that. Then some inner instinct warned him that he needed to force his listeners into a positive statement of agreement, rather than just a passive acceptance of his plans.

"Those who're ready to go to work at once," he said, "take a step forward."

There was a pause, a rustle of movement; then Vouhroi stood up. One by one and in groups they all rose from their chairs and stepped toward Miles.

"Good!" said Miles. He kept his voice calm, but triumph sang inside him. "Now let's find out what it takes to operate this ship and her weapons!" he said. "I'll go to the control room. With me will be Luhon as my second-in-command and Eff as my third-in-command. Chak'ha will join the rest of you on the weapons. Scatter around the ship now, find yourselves weapons, and try to warm them up."

Without waiting for any sign of assent from them, Miles turned and strode from the room toward the passageway, the corridor leading to the control room in the vessel's bow. He heard footfalls behind him and knew that Luhon, Eff, and Chak'ha were following, while a general confused sound of voices and movement behind him indicated that at least some of the rest of the crew were obeying. He led the way up into the control room and paused before the central of the three seats that faced the control console under the large vision screen with its view of the blackness of intergalactic space.

"We'll have to practice, too," he muttered, as much to himself as to the three others, who had followed him in.

"Shall I show you how, friend Miles?" murmured the soft voice of Luhon in his ear. Miles turned sharply to face the gray-skinned alien.

"Do you know something about this I don't?" Miles asked. "The information about these controls was evidently put into me by the Center Aliens when they first took me over."

"So it was in me—in all of us," answered Luhon, unperturbed. "But you have to remember I've fought with this ship thousands of times, and you haven't."

Miles stared at him. Another ripple of amusement sped from Luhon to break against Miles' perception.

"What do you think I've been doing up here all alone, all this time?" asked Luhon. "Thousands of times, in my imagination, I've fought this ship against the Silver Horde—never believing it would actually ever happen, that I would really fight her. You know the controls, friend Miles, as well as I do, but I know the *ship* better than you do."

The breath sighed suddenly from Miles' lungs. An empty feeling came to dwell suddenly in the area of his stomach. It had never occurred to him that they would not all be starting out as equals. How was he to keep Luhon as his second-in-command when the gray-skinned alien was not only his physical superior but his superior in experience of controlling the vessel, as well?

"No, friend Miles," said Luhon. Miles turned to see the brilliant eyes regarding him and realized that Luhon had read his emotional reaction with the same perceptiveness with which Miles and evidently everyone else aboard the ship had been equipped by the Center Aliens. Luhon's sensing of Miles' emotional reaction, plus a shrewd guess, could be tantamount to Luhon's reading Miles' mind. "Remember, you're the one who believes that we can get good enough to be allowed to fight the Silver Horde in our own persons. I still don't believe it, and if the power of this ship is really psychic rather than physical, that power is going to depend on someone who can *believe*."

Miles nodded. He sat down in the central control seat. Luhon took the seat to his right, and Eff slid into the seat at his left, as if at the order of some unspoken command.

"Suppose we lock in together as a single pattern, just the three of us to start," said Luhon calmly. "And I'll take the two of you on a computerized version of one of my imaginary battles."

His fingers flew over the controls of the console before him, and Miles found his own fingers flying as well. The consoles were identical—he already knew that from that information the Center Aliens had earlier planted in his mind. Each of them could control this ship independently, but there was a triangular reinforcement of purpose and strength if one individual and one console led and the other two followed and reinforced. Now, with Luhon leading but with the master controls still in off position so that the vessel did not actually fly or fight, Miles followed Luhon into the gray-skinned alien's imaginary battle against the Silver Horde. The ship, Miles realized as his fingers flashed over the controls, *could* be flown. But the weapons were dead—and not only because the crew of the *Fighting Rowboat* had ignored them all this time. Some master control of the Center Aliens held the weapons locked and useless.

But the psychic patterns, the emotional reflexes of Miles and his two companions, were joined together now into a single reacting unit. Their thoughts were not joined, but they reached in unison and with an automatic understanding of one another. They were welded into a single purpose and action. It was a strange feeling to Miles, for within Eff's share of that pattern Miles could now sense the direct, open, and vital quality of the bearlike alien, and in Luhon, at his right, he could sense the deep, dark-running feelings beneath the gentle exterior of soft voice and swift, silent movement. Just so, Miles now understood, the other two would be sensing *him* to a greater degree than they ever had previously.

Meanwhile, computer-created before them all, there had appeared on the vision screen before them the shape of a silver crescent in the light of the artificial sun over the battle line. A silver crescent, horns forward, pointing toward them. It was, Miles' Center Alien-implanted knowledge told him, a reconstructed image of what the Silver Horde had looked like attacking this galaxy a million years before.

Their fingers moved automatically on the consoles in response to their wishes. The instruments recorded the *Fighting Rowboat* as lifting from her position—even while in reality she still stayed where she was. In mock action, she was recorded as drifting outward to join the vanguard of other ships from the Battle Line advancing against the invaders.

Now the screen showed that advance. At the far left end of the advancing line was the tiny shape of the *Fighting Rowboat*. Even the ship next to her—the smallest of the great round ships of the Center Aliens—was many hundred times her size and mass.

Together, the galaxy's ships joined in formation, and faster now—and then faster—they plunged together toward the oncoming silver crescent of the attacking Horde.

The silver crescent shape was pulsing and swelling rapidly on the screen. Now it began to be visible in depth, if not in thickness, like a great flat scimitar swung at them in the same plane as their own battle line's formation. A few moments more, and its front edge began to fuzz, to reveal itself—as the two opposing armadas approached each other in shifts that must be many times the speed of light—as an incredible multitude of individual vessels.

Luhon stepped up the magnification on the screen. The view of the approaching front line of scout vessels of the Silver Horde jumped at them. They were small ships—even smaller than the *Fighting Rowboat* herself, which would have made three of them—but there were literally millions of them in this first line of invaders alone. A feeling of beserk joy leaped from the imagination of Luhon and communicated itself to Miles and Eff. In his

108

imagination the little *Fighting Rowboat* suddenly thrust with extra energy ahead of her huge partners until she alone was drawing away toward the enemy in advance of all the rest of the front line of galaxy ships.

On and on she plunged, faster and faster, now so far in advance of her former linemates that the big ships would not be able to support her during the moment in which she would first make contact with the oncoming scout ships of the Horde.

Their imaginations locked together with the imagination of Luhon, neither Miles nor Eff cared, as Luhon himself did not care. The white fury of battle lust that had flamed within each of them during their fights among themselves aboard the ship was now unified in the locked psychic pattern and was lashing them on against the Horde. To die was nothing. But to cut and slash and kill among the silver vessels—that was everything, no matter what the personal cost.

Now they were almost upon the scout ships. Now they were suddenly among them, striking right and left with their weapons—paralyzing the psychic opposition of the smaller invader vessels long enough to slash open the silver ships with the physical edge of their combined weapons. Like a wolf among a pack of weasels—in the imagination of Luhon—they raged right and left, up and down the oncoming wave of Horde scout ships, snapping, shaking, slashing, and killing.

But now the larger ships of the invaders, their second wave, were almost upon the *Fighting Rowboat*. It would take a miracle to manage their escape. But the imagination of Luhon had programmed the miracle into the exercise. In the nick of time, the *Fighting Rowboat* flung free and raced away—just as the heavy vessels of the Center Aliens came up to engage with the second wave of the Horde.

But the little vessel was not finished. Safe behind her own dreadnoughts, she turned again and hung around the outskirts of the conflict, snapping up those smaller vessels of the enemy that reeled hurt from the battle. She was still among the fury of it all when the Horde's crescent began to break up, began to drift away and re-form, moving in a different plane and line away from the galaxy. Mixed with the huge dreadnoughts of the Center Aliens, the *Fighting Rowboat* joined in harrying and driving away the defeated ships of the Silver Horde.

Suddenly Luhon's programmed battle ended. Suddenly the pattern of the three minds broke apart. Miles sat back exhausted in his seat and, looking about, saw Luhon and Eff slumped on either side of him.

For a long moment, even as he sagged exhausted in his seat before the console, the feeling of the imagined victory continued to glow inside Miles. But slowly that glow dwindled, flickered, and went out.

Of course, it was not true. It would not be like that. It could never be like that except in the self-indulgent imagination of one of them, like Luhon. Only in imagination could pygmies join in battle with giants without being destroyed. The lucky chances that had saved them time and again in Luhon's visualization of the attack in actual fact would not be. The *Fighting Rowboat* would get her chance to fight only at the price of almost certain destruction. That was something they all had to face.

Miles found himself facing it with a cold and settled determination. As the feeling of that determination solidified like some hard and massive diamond within the very core of his being, he felt the minds of Eff and Luhon linking with his in pattern once again, and he felt a comparable hardness of decision and determination in them.

Good. It was settled then. Now the center point of the three-mind pattern, Miles began instinctively to reach out. He reached out and drew into the pattern of three the fourth mind, that of Chak'ha, then that of Vouhroi, and so on down the line of weapons on each side of the ship, as the psychic pattern reached out to enclose all those aboard her.

The skill with which he did this was clearly another of the abilities that the Center Aliens had given him. He had not suspected that he had it until he used it. But now that he had used it, he became suddenly conscious of how little the Center Aliens had expected it to be used in this way before the moment in which the larger pattern of the total battle line should activate them all as part of itself. Now, however, the pattern had set itself up alone in the minds of

110

them all as one unit aboard the ignored and overlooked tiny *Fighting Rowboat*. A fierce and angry pride kindled within the pattern, and Miles was not sure whether he was its kindling point or not. But as the heat of that feeling spread out among them all, it illuminated within each individual the same hard, diamondlike core of decision to fight, even at the cost of dying, that Miles had found in himself, Luhon, and Eff.

They were barbarians in the sight of the Center Aliens. A thousand bloody, primitive battle cries out of their near and savage ancestry clamored in the mind and memory of each one of the twenty-three who was now locked in the pattern. They clamored also in the brain of Miles, at the leading point of that trianglelike pattern. Out of that welter of recalled sound a single phrase he had once read leaped clear and plain into his mind. No proud and noble speech of the battlefield, but the grim and sordid chorus rising from the bloody sand of the arena. The onetime salute of the gladiators of imperial Rome to Rome's Emperor: *Morituri te salutamus!*

"We who are about to die salute thee!"

11

The weapons did not warm up quickly. Somewhere in their combined physical and psychic mechanism was some sort of minimum operating level of potency. Until each weapon was warmed by the response of an intelligent mind to a certain value or effectiveness, it would not be capable of working, even if the Center Aliens should unlock the firing mechanism. It was three weeks before they had all the guns on the vessel capable of responding—in theory—when Miles should call upon them for mass fire.

Meanwhile, the actual approaching Silver Horde had been sighted. It was not yet visible on the vision screen in the control room of the *Fighting Rowboat,* but a pale ring of light circled the spot on the screen where it would first become visible. Even this much was like a stimulant to the twenty-three aboard the *Fighting Rowboat.* They worked eagerly now with their weapons and the ship—dry-firing,

111

for the weapons remained locked. But that fact made little difference. As far as the feedback of response from weapon to the one man handling it was concerned, the feeling was the same as if he had actually used it against one of the ships of the Silver Horde.

With Miles now in command, they also practiced actually lifting the ship from its platform, running half a dozen light-years out beyond the Battle Line, and there slashing at the computer-created enemy.

The computer element itself was evidently a smaller version of those large calculative mechanisms which they had been taught to understand were possessed by the Center Aliens in their enormous ships. It would be those larger computers which, calculating up until the last moment before the attack of the Horde, would decide whether opposition would be worthwhile or whether it would not be better for the warships assembled here to break up and run, to hide and try to survive—so that they might protect what few worlds were ignored, from stragglers and small hunting parties of the silver invaders. The small computer aboard the *Fighting Rowboat*, however, would have no hand in this decision. But it could be used like this to program an imaginary attack of the Silver Horde, calling on the crew of the spaceship to repulse it. More than this, it could rate their performance.

In the several weeks that followed that first takeoff, with all guns now operating, in dry-fire at least, the computer aboard the *Fighting Rowboat* charted a steady increase in the ability and effectiveness of the ship and crew. However, as the line marking their progress mounted on the chart, it began to level off. Soon it became plain that they were approaching a plateau of skill. Miles, Luhon, and Eff sat down together to figure out what might be the problem that was keeping them from progressing further.

"I don't understand it," said Luhon, as they sat together in the control room of the ship, in conference. The ship lay on its platform, and the rest of the crew had abandoned their weapons for rest after a long session of dry-firing and simulated battle. "We've all handled those weapons at one time or another. You can feel there's no theoretical limit to the psychic energies those weapons can take from us. There couldn't be, because whatever we can

112

feed into them, it's going to be many times multiplied when the full psychic pattern of the total Battle Line locks in and takes over."

"It's plain enough," Eff put in. "It's not the weapons that're at fault. It has to be us. For some reason it looks as if we're reaching the limit of our capabilities. But I don't believe that."

"I don't either," said Miles thoughtfully. "As I understand it, from the information the Center Aliens put in me when they changed me—check me on this, both of you—any individual's psychic power is like the power of any one of his muscles. Continual exercise should increase psychic power, just as it increases muscle power. All right, eventually maybe a limit has to be reached, depending on individual capacity, but it doesn't *feel* to me that we ought to be reaching ours this quickly. Do you two feel the same?"

"It checks," said Luhon briefly. His pointed ears twitched restlessly. "If those Center Aliens were halfway decent, we could get in touch with them and ask them what's wrong. But they wouldn't be interested in helping us."

"Maybe they couldn't," said Miles thoughtfully.

The other two looked at him curiously.

"What we may be having trouble with"—Miles hesitated—"may be outside their experience. Either because it's something they've never run up against. Or because it's something they had so far back in their own history that they've forgotten what it was like. Look— these Center Aliens can get many more times the effectiveness out of one of those weapons than one of us can. The one I talked to told me that he had more power in himself than all of us on this ship put together."

"I can believe it," said Luhon. "But I don't see any help in knowing that."

"It suggests something," said Miles.

"What?" asked Eff.

"Well," said Miles, "obviously, we're different from the Center Aliens. Maybe it's the difference that's tripping us up. Suppose we ask ourselves just how we *are* different."

Eff gave his short bark of a laugh.

"We're barbarians," he said. "They told us that."

113

"That's right," said Miles. "So maybe it's some barbarian quality of ours that's getting in the way of our doing better with these weapons." He glanced from Eff to Luhon and back again. "What do you think?"

"Well," Luhon began slowly, "we don't have their knowledge, obviously. But as I understand it, it isn't knowledge that feeds the psychic force. It's"—again he hesitated—"something like the spirit in the individual."

"Spirit, that's it! The whole emotional pattern we have!" said Miles. He looked closely at Luhon. "You see what I think I see, in that direction?"

Luhon's ears flicked. He stared back without answering.

"I don't see anything at all," put in Eff.

"Wait a minute," said Luhon slowly. "Miles, you mean that something about our emotional pattern is holding us back?" Abruptly he stiffened in his chair. "Of course —they don't react the way we do! They don't lose their tempers. They don't. . . ."

His voice trailed off thoughtfully.

"That's what I mean," said Miles. "We get wound up, self-intoxicated on our own emotion, when we fight. The Center Aliens don't." He paused and glanced at Eff and Luhon again, holding them both in his gaze. "Maybe our trouble's just that—intoxication, this battle fury of ours that keeps us from making better use of the weapons."

"But if that's it—" Luhon broke off sharply. "What're we going to do about it?"

"Practice," answered Miles harshly. "That's what we can do. Practice using the weapons without getting worked up about it. I know it won't be easy to do," he went on as Luhon opened his mouth to speak again, "but we can try—and maybe we can break through what's blocking us this way."

"There's always the possibility," Eff put in, "that the plateau of effectiveness we're on is something temporary. Maybe after staying at a constant level for a little while, we'll break out and start another stretch of improvement."

"The Silver Horde has already been indicated on the far instruments," retorted Miles bluntly. "Do you want to mark time and take the chance?"

Eff hesitated, then slowly shook his head.

"You're right, Miles," said Luhon. "Time's too short.

We've got to experiment. When do you want to try this business of operating the weapons without emotional involvement?"

"Right now," said Miles evenly. "And I'll tell you why. Right now we're all dead tired. It should make it that much easier to damp out our emotional reactions."

Eff laughed. Luhon spun about and sounded the signal throughout the ship that summoned all crew members to their battle stations. The gray-skinned alien gave the slight body twitch that was his symptom of amusement.

"They'll enjoy this," he said. He began announcing Miles' plan to the ship.

Meanwhile, Miles was calling on the computer element of the little ship for another simulated attack of the Silver Horde. It was not merely the rest of the crew that was weary. He, Luhon, and Eff were weary as well. As he lifted the ship from the platform and headed out into the interstellar darkness, he deliberately relaxed the tension that searching for an answer to their problem had built within him, and he felt weariness flood through him like a depressant drug.

It was several hours before they brought the ship back to her platform and had a chance to examine the computer's rating of their performance. It was down, of course, from what they had been scoring, but the interesting thing was that it was several points above what the computer calculated it should be with their weariness fed in as part of the performance equation.

Triumph fought with exhaustion within Miles. He heard Luhon's voice beside him and turned.

"Friend Miles," said Luhon, his eyes burning into Miles, "I think you've found the answer!"

Wearily they straggled off to their bunks. And the whole ship rested.

The next emotionless trial run that they held after that was a fiasco. The rested minds of the twenty-three aboard the *Fighting Rowboat* could not contain their emotional reactions, and the results were wildly spotty—highly successful in the case of some individuals, diastrous in the case of some others. But they kept at it until they had once again reached the stage of weariness they had reached on the first occasion.

115

With weariness, the individual performances evened out. But the total performance was still less than their previous best. Stubbornly Miles clung to the possibility that, with practice, they would be able to hold their emotions down and break free of the plateau after sufficient practice.

So it finally turned out. By the time the Silver Horde was close enough to show as a small bright dot in the midst of the control room vision screen, the general performance of the twenty-three was well above the earlier plateau and still climbing.

By the time the Silver Horde was identifiable as a small crescent shape in the control room screen the ship's computer showed that they had tripled their fighting effectiveness from what it had been at the plateau level.

It was time, thought Miles, for the Center Aliens to be told. Once the Center Aliens saw what the *Fighting Rowboat* could do, they could no longer reasonably withhold permission for the little ship to join the vessels actually engaging the Silver Horde.

He left word with Luhon of what he intended to do, took the small ship that was parked on the platform, and once more headed in toward the center of the Battle Line.

This time he did not make it even to within sight of the first great globe-shaped ship of the Center Aliens before one of them appeared beside him in the other seat of the little craft he was piloting.

"You have been told once," said the Center Alien calmly, but with a cold note in his voice, "that you were not to leave the immediate neighborhood of your ship and its platform. Such incursions must cease—"

He broke off abruptly and gazed steadily at Miles.

"Oh, I see," he went on in the same calm tone. "So you think that this situation now is somehow different?"

"Not only different but entirely new—for you, as well as us!" said Miles.

"No," said the Center Alien. "That is not possible. It is symptomatic of your lack of knowledge that you think that you might have discovered or produced anything outside our knowledge."

116

"We've become an effective fighting ship," said Miles slowly, unyielding. "We only ask you to come and see for yourselves."

The alien gazed at him for a moment without speaking.

"Suppose this were true," said the Center Alien. "Suppose that you actually had done the impossible and had qualified for a place among the fighting ships. Do you realize that if you joined in the actual battle, there would be no real possibility your ship could survive even the first contact with the Horde?"

"We understand that," said Miles.

"But still you want to throw your lives away in a gesture that can have little or no profit for you, let alone for the rest of the galaxy?" replied the Center Alien. "That in itself is a reasonless, emotion-laden reaction to a situation too large for you to comprehend. Since your basic reaction is flawed by emotion, how can any improvement that has come out of it be superior to that emotion?"

Miles opened his mouth, but there was no answer immediately ready to his tongue.

"You see," said the Center Alien, and under his hands the small boat turned about and began to head back once more toward the end of the line where the *Fighting Rowboat* waited, "you see yourself how you have stated an impossibility. A creature without wings may practice jumping in the air and flapping his limbs to the point where he can jump higher and flap harder—but this is not flying and never will be."

Miles found his voice at last. His voice and his argument.

"I see," he said, "you're never wrong—not even on a statistical basis?"

"Of course—on a statistical basis, we can be wrong," answered the Center Alien.

"Then there has to be a chance you're wrong about us now," said Miles.

"Of course," replied the Center Alien, "there is always a chance—but a chance too small to merit practical consideration."

"Still," said Miles grimly, "no matter how small that chance is, with the galaxy facing a fight for its life, you owe it to yourself and us at least to examine what we've done, to see if even that infinitely small chance may not be fact."

The Center Alien continued to pilot the little ship onward, back toward the end of the line. But he did not seem to Miles to be thinking so much as communicating with some one or ones elsewhere.

Without warning, Miles found himself no longer in the little ship. Instead, he and a Center Alien in human form, who looked like the same one who had just been sitting beside him in the small craft, now stood in an area—it was hard to call it a room—that was walled and floored and ceilinged with shimmering yellow light. Directly before them in one wall a milky blue and white globe seemed either to float or to spin at an incredible speed.

It hurt Miles' eyes to watch the globe. He looked away toward the steadily flowing yellow light of the wall, which was more bearable. Swarming in suddenly upon the heightened perceptivity that the aliens had given him came an impingement, a feeling of being surrounded on all sides by many minds. All at once he realized that he was inside—literally inside—one of the huge ships of the Center Aliens.

"You will look at——" The last word said by the Center Alien had meanings beyond the ability of Miles' mind to grasp. It translated vaguely in his mind as words like "eye" or "window." But he understood that it was the globe to which the Center Alien referred.

He forced his eyes back to the globe, which caught and held his gaze with a strength and intensity that were so great as to be almost painful. He felt himself, his mind, his memories, everything about him, being in some way *examined*.

For a long moment the examination continued. Then, abruptly, it was over. He found himself free to look again at the yellow, flowing light of the walls, which he did gratefully.

"It is settled then," said the voice of the Center Alien beside him. "You will be given the observational test for which you've asked."

Abruptly he was back in the small ship. The Center Alien sat beside him again, and they were still headed back toward the end of the line where the *Fighting Rowboat* waited on her platform.

No, *they* were not headed back. Looking sideways at the Center Alien beside him and feeling the emotional response under the illusory appearance of humanity that clothed him, Miles sensed that this was a different individual from the Center Alien who had first picked him up.

Miles opened his mouth to comment on this and then closed it again. They rode in silence back to the platform where the *Fighting Rowboat* waited.

However, when they left the small ship and Miles started up the ladder into the *Fighting Rowboat,* he became conscious of the fact that the Center Alien was not following him. Turning about, halfway up the ladder, he saw the Center Alien standing still on the platform about a dozen steps off.

"Go ahead," said the Center Alien. "I will observe from here."

Miles went on up the ladder and closed the entrance port of the *Fighting Rowboat* behind him. The air of tension and excitement within struck him like a physical blow. He stalked rapidly through the lounge and into the control room, where Eff and Luhon were already in their seats. Their faces looked a question at him, but he did not answer that question to them, alone. Instead, he sat down in his own seat before the central console and, touching a communications control, spoke to everyone aboard the ship.

"Calm down," he said. "All of you, calm yourselves. We can't put on any demonstration, keyed up the way we are now. I'm giving everybody two minutes to damp down his emotions. Remember we're under observation here, and we're going to be judged from the moment we lift off the platform."

He dropped his finger from the control and sat back limply in his chair, trying to relax. He did not look to either right or left at his two underofficers. Before him on the console, a chronometer marked off those secondlike sections of time which made up intervals roughly analogous to Earth Minutes.

As he sat there, Miles could feel his own tension lowering like the red line of the spirit level in a thermometer plunged into ice water on a warm day. Not only that, but—he could feel now—the general air of tension in the vessel was also slipping away. At the end of two minutes those aboard the *Fighting Rowboat* were almost calm.

Miles touched the controls, and the ship lifted. For a moment he wondered how the Center Alien was going to observe them when they would be light-years out from the Battle Line in intergalactic darkness. But that was the Center Alien's worry. He dismissed the thought and put his whole mind to handling the craft.

The emotion of the twenty-three aboard the ship had evaporated now. There was left only the hard purpose—the hard, cold purpose—of their intentness on the exercise. The *Fighting Rowboat* was now a good dozen light-years out in front of the rest of the Battle Line. Miles pressed a control on the console before him. The illusory Silver Horde ships that were the first phase of their battle exercise were produced by the computer on the screen before him and on the screens that were the transparent bubbles enclosing the weapons lining the ship's sides.

Miles' hands leaped over the console before him, and the hands of Luhon and Eff followed him on either side as the small ship flung itself against its smaller, imaginary enemies, some fifteen or twenty of the Silver Horde's scout ships backed up by one of the ships of the Horde's second line, which was several times as large and with many times the firepower. As they closed with the imaginary enemy under Miles' direction, the *Fighting Rowboat* altered direction, using her mobility, which was greater than that of the second-line Horde ship, to keep a screen of Horde scout ships always between herself and the superior weapons of the second-line ship. As she did so, the *Fighting Rowboat*'s own weapons flashed outward, killing off the enemy scout ships one by one.

Then, when the number of enemy scout ships was down to only four, the *Fighting Rowboat* turned and fled, having done a maximum amount of damage to the ships she was able to kill, and having held up for a number of precious moments a larger ship that she was not able to destroy. In theory, the Horde second-line ship, delayed in this way, should have been a sitting duck for the larger ships on the galactic side that were able to outgun it. The total effect of the exercise had demonstrated, in theory, an effectiveness in the *Fighting Rowboat* that was better than three times what she had possessed originally.

Glowing with inner triumph, Miles turned the small vessel back toward the platform. Inside him was a sort of quiet pride for the other twenty-two aboard. Not one of them had broken emotional discipline. They had remained as cool-headed and objective about their fighting as—Miles thought—any Center Alien would have done.

They headed back to their platform, but as they approached it and hovered ready to land on it, something materialized below them.

It was a Horde scout ship.

This had not been in the programmed exercise. But reflex took over. Miles hit the alarm control, even as the Silver Horde scout ship leaped into the air from the platform. A sudden explosion of emotion from the rest of the twenty-three—all coolness forgotten—struck Miles like a physical blow, even as their weapons opened fire on the scout ship.

But even as they commenced to fire, the scout ship vanished—and hanging there in space before them was the small, unprotected figure of the Center Alien who had been observing them. His eyes met Miles' through the vision screen—and something like a solid blow seemed to strike Miles from within.

It clove through the reflex of white, raging battle fury within him. It froze him, abruptly paralyzed and with a mind suddenly empty of decision. His hand hovered above the controls but did not drop to touch them.

About him, the weapons of the *Fighting Rowboat* were silent. Miles felt his hands moved then, as if by some outside force.

His fingers descended stiffly on the controls, and he brought the *Fighting Rowboat* back down onto her berth on the platform.

Looking out through his screen, once they were down on the platform, Miles saw the Center Alien standing where he had stood before, obviously waiting. Miles rose from his seat before the console, turned, and walked out alone. Around him and behind him as he left it, the other twenty-two who manned the ship were silent, still in their places, locked there by the shock of defeat. Miles walked down the corridor, out the now-open hatch, and down the ladder, which had slid itself out as the hatch was opened. He approached the Center Alien and stopped only a few feet from him. His eyes met the eyes in the apparently human face of the Center Alien.

"So you see," said the Center Alien coldly. "There are stages to the development of a civilized, intelligent race. Once we too were like you. We had the old, savage instincts still in us. But we came to the point where we could deliberately rid ourselves of those instincts—as you would amputate a diseased limb. And then we went on to develop other skills."

He paused, looking at Miles. Miles could think of nothing to say.

"Naturally," said the Center Alien, "you have the barbarian's instinct to fight when you are attacked. But do not confuse that instinct with *ability* to fight—which, by comparison with ourselves, you do not have."

He vanished. Miles stood numbly staring at the blank platform where the other had stood.

12

On the *Fighting Rowboat,* they had come during their weeks of training to believe that they had improved to the point of being at least half equal to the Center Aliens, individual for individual. Now a Center Alien had stopped all twenty-three of them cold, with nothing more than his own personal psychic force. The effect on the twenty-three was crushing.

It did not matter that he had tricked them, with the appearance of a Horde scout ship where no Horde scout ship should be, into letting loose their primitive emotions of battle lust and fury. For if he could make them betray themselves that easily, it was plain that they would betray themselves before the Horde. They had been tricked into proving their own worthlessness by their own instinctive actions, and the knowledge of that worthlessness lay like a bitterness in the pit of the stomach of each.

Their contempt and anger were not turned against the Center Alien who had made them betray themselves. They were turned against themselves—and against Miles. When Miles returned to the ship after his last words with the Center Alien observer, it was as if he had stepped back into a cage of wild beasts, all prowling about with downcast eyes, apparently not looking at him, but waiting only for the smallest movement or sound on his part that could be used as an excuse for an attack.

Grimly, he gave them no excuse. He knew them now, after these weeks of working together, and he knew that the worst thing he could do at this time would be to urge them to go back on their training. Deliberately, except for Chak'ha, who alone had not deserted him, he ignored them and went back to his self-training at the control console, alone. Day after day he worked there, while the dot that was the Silver Horde grew steadily on the control room vision screen.

And slowly, having nothing else to fight, nothing else to do, the rest of the twenty-three began to return. First Luhon, then Eff, then gradually other members of the crew came to join Miles in the control room, standing behind him and silently watching the screen as he watched it. As Miles had gambled they would, those emotions which had betrayed them as barbarians before the Center Alien observer now began to take hold of them once again whether they wished it or not. For this reaction, too, was predictable and instinctive.

The Silver Horde was plainly visible on the screen in all its numbers now—right down to the last line of rearguard vessels. Those in the control room with Miles watched with him as the individual lines of silver ships, the individual squadrons of the Horde's advance, seemed to surge forward individually, then stop, then surge and stop again. In order, like muscles rippling down the many ribs of a moving snake, the Horde came on by shift steps, moving light-years at a shift, through the dark vastness beyond the galaxy's spiral arm. Already its total fleet filled nearly a hundred and twenty degrees of the hundred and eighty degrees of screen. It was a silver mass, thick at the center and thinning out toward the ends with the tips of its line curving forward like horns, ready to encircle any world or solar system or fleet that offered resistance or sustenance to the millions within its silver ships.

Watching it sent a cold feeling, like a chilling draft, across the back of Miles' neck. By this time the Horde was plainly aware of the Battle Line that was waiting for it and, far from avoiding it, its fleet had clearly altered course to meet the Battle Line head on. Early in the fourth week following the *Fighting Rowboat*'s failure before the Center Alien observer, this shift in course became obvious to Miles, and during the rest of the week it began to penetrate the minds of the rest of the crew.

With that penetration, a strange thing began to happen aboard the *Fighting Rowboat*.

Without consultation, in fact almost with a silent, unanimous consent, the twenty-three began to take up their old duties aboard the ship, and, again without consultation, Miles one day found himself with Eff and Luhon seated on either side of him, lifting the *Fighting Rowboat* once more from the platform for a training session.

They ran through a programmed attack without a flaw, and with no trace of that emotion that had betrayed them at the hand of the Center Alien observer. In fact, there was a new air of cold purpose aboard the ship. They all felt it, but Miles most of all. To him, as leader, it felt as if a powerful hand had been laid between his shoulder blades, shoving him irresistibly forward into rehearsal after rehearsal for the attack that was coming.

In fact, there was a new closeness about them all aboard the *Fighting Rowboat*. The approach of the Horde served to gather up the fragments of their collective spirit and weld it back together again into one solid mass— harder now because it had been tempered by what they had been through.

Their efficiency and potency with the weapons climbed sharply. By the time the Horde was less than a week from decision point—that moment in which retreat would be no longer possible for the ships of the Battle Line—Miles' rating charts showed the *Fighting Rowboat* to have more than doubled her effectiveness since the time the Center Alien had come to observe them.

"But they'll still never agree to let us fight," said Eff, standing beside Miles as he checked the last point of advance on the chart. "We're still only animals to them.

124

Useful because they can drink our blood before the battle to make themselves strong for it. But aside from that, we're just so many cattle to be left behind when the real action comes!"

"Still, anything can happen," answered Luhon softly from Miles' other side. "Maybe the Horde will decide whether we fight them or not. Maybe the decision won't be up to the Center Aliens once the real fighting starts."

Miles said nothing. But he understood the other two, just as he understood the new, welded singleness of decision of all aboard the *Fighting Rowboat*. The other twenty-two had come to the point he himself had reached a long time ago. They had stopped trying to reconcile the powerful, undeniable feelings burning within them with the cold and distant attitude of the Center Aliens. Now they simply disregarded the fact that the Center Aliens had refused them the right to fight when the battle was joined. They ignored that refusal and continued to prepare themselves as though their part in that battle were inevitable.

Meanwhile, the Horde came on.

13

Three days until Decision Point.

Two days.

One. Miles got up from his seat before the control console and the vision screen. He walked back through the ship, past the rest of the twenty-two. They sat, silently working with their weapons. Miles went alone out onto the platform.

He looked off into the direction in which the Horde was coming.

But here, to the naked eye, there was nothing to see. The silver ships were still buried in intergalactic darkness, light-years distant and invisible still.

Here there was nothing but the shape of the *Fighting Rowboat,* silent under the distant light of the artificial sun overlooking the Battle Line, and the storage shed, motionless on the glinting metal deck of the platform. Miles looked to his right.

Dimly, off there in airlessness, was a little reflection—a faint gleam from the small ship next to the *Fighting Rowboat*. He turned around.

Behind him stretched the long line of misty whiteness that was the spiral of the galaxy he was here to defend, now shrunk to a spindle shape, so distant that the shape of the Earth he had come from was more than dwindled into invisibility—it had become a part of a whole.

He turned back to look out again into the darkness where the powerful eye of the vision screen had told him that the Horde was rushing down on him at translight speeds. Just hours and minutes away now—and still invisible to the unaided vision.

He chilled at the massiveness of the scene compared to his own smallness as he stood here between the glowing line of the uncounted stars of his galaxy and the uncounted ships of the invisible Horde—part of one single Battle Line of which his ship was the last and least.

Here, as he stood on the platform by the silent ship, it seemed to him suddenly that none of it was real —Horde, galaxy, or Battle Line. Either that or he had been caught in a dispute between things huge and invisible and placed out here to be crushed by the clash of their meeting. . . .

He turned and went slowly back across the platform, up the ladder, and back into the ship. He went back up the corridor to the control room, where Luhon and Eff still sat in their seats before their controls, gazing at the screen, and he took the empty commander's seat between them.

He looked at the screen.

It had been extended now, curved forward through forty-five degrees at each end to encompass the full picture of the Horde as it was now seen from the viewpoint of their ship in the Battle Line. Now, in the directionless blackness of intergalactic space, it no longer seemed to be coming at them horizontally.

It had expanded to fill the expanded screen horizontally and stretch into the screen additions with the hornlike tips of its forward-curving ends, but it had expanded as well in its middle section to fill the center screen from top to bottom. Now it seemed to be not so much ahead of them as above them, hanging over them, rushing down on them like some great voracious amoeba, pulsing with life in the successive shifts of its successive lines of ships, its horntip arms already stretching forward to enclose them and cut off retreat.

"Those armtips must be level with us now, don't you think?" said Luhon, echoing Miles' own unspoken thought. All of the twenty-three aboard the ship had seemed to think with one mind lately. Luhon punched controls on the console before him, requesting a calculation.

After a moment the result flickered on the small console screen. He touched the wipe-out button.

"Yes," he said. "Theoretically, they've got ships behind us now."

"How long to Decision Point?" asked Miles.

"Five hours, some minutes," said Eff.

Time went by. Now it was just four and a half hours to Decision Point. . . .

Four hours to Decision Point. . . .

Three. . . .

Two. . . .

One hour. Thirty minutes. . . .

"What's the matter with them?" snarled Eff. For once his cheerful, bearlike face was all animal fury. "What are they waiting for? What's going to happen that's new in the next few minutes—"

"*Attention!*" The communications speaker above them broke suddenly into life with the flat, passionless voice of a Center Alien. "Attention! Your weapons are now unlocked, ready to be used. You will leave the Battle Line immediately, head back into the galaxy, and attempt to find a hiding place around or on some world of a system that does not possess organic life. I will repeat that. Your ship's weapon controls and weapons are now unlocked. You are to leave the Battle Line immediately, return to the galaxy, and hide yourselves on some lifeless solar system."

The voice ceased as suddenly as it had begun. So quietly had it spoken, so abruptly had it stopped speaking, that it was a few seconds before Miles and the others were able to react. Then a wave of common emotion—felt along that network of emotional sensitivity that enclosed them all—swept throughout the ship like a silent moan of disbelief and new fury.

"They're sending us away," whispered Luhon. His eyes were glittering. "They can't do that to us."

"That's right," said Miles in a voice he hardly recognized as his own. "They can't!"

He was already busy, jabbing at the call button of the communicator in front of him.

"Answer me!" he snapped into the voice grille of the console before him. "Answer me! I'm calling for an answer!"

But there was no answer. Miles continued to call and jab at the button until at last his hand dropped in defeat.

"They won't answer," he muttered. For a moment he sat without moving; then at a sudden thought, his hand leaped out again to punch for a picture of the Battle Line, stretching away to their right.

It took shape on the screen in front of him. He pulled back the focus until he was able to see several dozen of the ships stretching off to the right. As he watched, one of the ships disappeared—it had gone into shift.

A moment later, the ship only two stations up from the *Fighting Rowboat* also blinked out and disappeared.

Miles felt coldness flood through him on a wave of icy shock.

"They can't be," he muttered to himself. "They can't—"

"Can't what?" snapped Luhon.

But Miles' fingers had jumped once more to the communications section of the console in front of him.

"This is the last ship in line!" Miles was snapping into the microphone grill. "This is the last ship in line, calling the ship sixth up from our position. Are you preparing to leave the Battle Line? Answer me! Are you preparing to leave the Battle Line? If so, why? Why? Answer me—"

"We hear you," interrupted the overhead speaker suddenly in the common language of those aboard the *Fighting Rowboat* but in harsh, unfamiliar accents. "Yes, we are leaving. We are retreating with the rest. Why do you ask?"

"Retreating?" echoed Miles. "Retreating—you mean

just we little ships are retreating? Or more than just us?"

"Haven't you been informed?" roared the harsh voice above him. "The Center's computational devices have said that all should save themselves. The devices have calculated and found an answer that predicts defeat if we try to stop the Horde. All are leaving. All—"

The voice was cut off suddenly, as Miles jabbed at both voice and sight communication controls. Abruptly, in the screen before them formed a schema of the whole Battle Line. It showed the line from end to end and the ships in all their sizes and varieties, but as if only a few yards were separating them. As Miles, Luhon, and Eff watched, ships were winking out of existence in that line. Even the huge globular dreadnoughts of the Center Aliens were disappearing.

It was true. After everything—after all their work and the work of the Center Aliens and others to set up this Battle Line—now just because of some cold answer given by a lifeless mechanism, the greatest strength the galaxy could gather was not going to face the Horde after all. They all were going to turn tail and run, save themselves, and let the Horde in to feed on the helpless worlds they had been sent out here to protect.

"My people," breathed Luhon.

His head flashed out with that fantastic speed of reflex he possessed, and without warning, on the screen before them all was the picture of the Horde again, like some evil, glittering silver amoeba, hanging over them all, reaching out as if to swallow not only the former Battle Line but the whole galaxy behind it in one vast and evil embrace.

Before Miles, in that moment, there also rose up a picture of his people and his world—the world as he had seen it during those last days when he had moved like a ghost from spot to spot about its surface and among its many people. He saw it, and at the same time in his mind's eye he saw the picture of the world that the two Center Aliens had shown him—a world that a million years before had been cleaned to the point of barrenness by the Horde.

In his mind's eye now he saw Earth like that. One endless, horizon-wide strength of naked earth and soil, with nothing left. Everything gone—all gone. The cities, the people within them, their history, their music, their paintings, Marie Bourtel. . . .

"I won't!"

It was more than a verbal shout, it was a roar within the very fibers of his being. A roar of no-saying to all that the Horde represented and to all that retreat without any attempt to stop the invaders would mean. It was an answer to the idea that he, Miles, could go and hide himself while the Horde swept off, possibly to do to Earth what it had done to that other, unknown world a million years ago. There was nothing intellectual or sensible about that great roar of negation that picked him up body, mind, and soul, like a whirlwind. It was as deep and basic within him as the ancient, unconquerable savagery that used to reach out and destroy the intent of his paintings.

And it was echoed around him through the emotional matrix enclosing the twenty-two other savage beings who shared this ship with him. Like him, they were reacting without the need for thought, and there was now not even a need for consultation.

Miles' hands slapped down on the console in front of him. To his right, Luhon's flashing gray fingers were already blurring over his controls, and Eff was busy at his left.

Like a single living creature, with one mind alone, the *Fighting Rowboat* lifted from her cradle and flashed into shift—single-handedly and alone into attack against the uncountable numbers of the Silver Horde.

14

Alarm bells shrilled. Signal lights on the board before Miles flared in bright silver warning. On the screen the great rippling mass of the Horde seemed unchanged—but the instruments signaled that the invaders had taken note of the little ship's attack and were even now ponderously beginning to swing about to face this one end of the former Battle Line, from which a lone attacker had come.

The massiveness of that shift in itself had something blindly elemental about it, as if the Horde were actually nothing but some vast amoeba reacting blindly to the presence of prey.

But the *Fighting Rowboat* was closing the distance between her and the nearest of the silver enemy scout ships at a rate beyond mental calculation. Automatic devices aboard the little boat had taken over now. Each shift was shorter than the one before. With each she was zeroing in on that front line of silver, minnowlike attackers. Shortly the last shift would bring her out at almost a matched velocity and direction. She would then be running side by side with the first wave of scout ships, headed back toward the galaxy.

Meanwhile, aboard the *Fighting Rowboat* a new sense of grim unity thrummed through them all. Not only did they feel one another in the common network of sensitivity. It seemed to Miles that they went beyond this, into the unlocked weapons themselves. The weapons seemed like quasi-living things now; Miles felt them against his mind like the touch of the console keys against his fingertips.

He felt more. Beyond the weapons he felt the ship. Now even she seemed alive, driven by the fury of their response to the alien attack. Like a single cornered animal, the *Fighting Rowboat* hurled herself at the invaders.

The shifts were very small now. They had almost ended. . . . They had ended.

Abruptly, the *Fighting Rowboat* found herself in black space, with the light of the artificial sun that the Center Aliens had hung over the Battle Line dwindling to a tiny bright dot behind her. And around the crew, on instruments and on screen, the scout ships of the Silver Horde finally registered—each one no more than a third the size of the *Fighting Rowboat*, but within the *Fighting Rowboat*'s vicinity they numbered in the dozens.

In the light of the distant artificial sun Miles could even see the two closest, as gleams of dull silver, seen briefly, like the soft flash of the pale belly of a fish glimmering for a moment up through deep water.

Miles' hands came down on the controls, and the *Fighting Rowboat* flung herself at the nearest pale gleam.

Now the whole crew was aware of the working psychic elements. Now, through their weapons, they could finally feel the alien minds of the weasel-shaped members of the Horde aboard the nearest scout ships. The consciousness of the aliens was like a small, hard fist pushing back at the strength that enclosed and emanated from the *Fighting Rowboat*.

That bubble of strength flowed over and encapsulated the alien consciousnesses aboard the scout boats within weapon range. Miles, with the others, felt how they held the scout members of the Horde will-less within their bubble of psychic power.

They had done it. The closer scout ships were drifting helplessly, their crews paralyzed. Luhon's quick fingers danced over the firing-control buttons before him, and from the weapons of the *Fighting Rowboat* pale sighting beams reached out to touch the scout ships—and a second later there stabbed down the center of those sighting beams a force which ripped open the enemy vessels.

The *Fighting Rowboat* struck, and moved, and struck again. . . . Suddenly they were in a little open space. They were through the first line of scout ships.

They had won. At least in this first contact.

A furious feeling of triumph rolled through their network of common sensitivity. They had struck the enemy and lived. Their savage souls exulted at the thought.

But now, plainly before them on the screen and swiftly closing down about them, were the second-line scout ships of the Horde, and these were each half again as big as the *Fighting Rowboat*.

The next contact was one they could not win. But their ancient instincts hurled them forward.

Abruptly then, it happened—for a *third* time to Miles.

As it had when his painting had been stolen and he had climbed the cliff, as it had when he was fighting with Chak'ha, so it happened once more now. He went into hysterical strength. Into overdrive.

Suddenly it was on him again—like a motor, relieved of the governor that had artificially limited its potential power, winding itself up tight to full output. He felt all of one piece, and strength raced through him. Now he knew without thinking about it that the two other beings sitting beside him at the controls would be no match for him in any physical encounter. The Horde had evoked it again in him—this final *overdrive* of strength. It seethed within him. He could almost feel it churning and frothing, searching for the needed physical violence that would provide it with a necessary point of escape.

But there was no such point. His physical strength was not needed here—the ship was his muscles. All that was left for him to do here was push buttons, and that he could have done with the ordinary strength that was in him. His arms and legs ached to be in action, but there was no job for them—only the small, easy tasks they were already doing. A feeling of frustration, wild and furious as a storm at sea, began to build to hurricane force inside him.

All the while, the *Fighting Rowboat* was closing with those larger ships of the Horde which must finally destroy her. And here sat Miles, tapping a great reservoir of strength in himself for which there was no use.

The storm mounted in him. It shook his whole body, so that his arms and legs trembled. His vision blurred. He felt as if he were tearing himself apart with a wild urge to greater action.

The overdrive power boiled within him, like a whirlpool of force, like a circular river seeking an outlet and hemmed in by tall mountains. It raced faster, still faster, seeking an outlet—and then, suddenly, he found it.

It was like a pass through the mountains leading to a higher land. It was a release for the explosive, whirling power building within him—but it was something more. It was, at this last moment before his own certain destruction, that which he had always searched for in his painting. An overdrive of the creative spirit, comparable to the overdrive of hysterical strength in the physical body.

In the same moment in which he recognized this, the pent-up force within him went pouring through its new-found outlet. It flashed through and upward, leaving his body at peace but switching his intellectual centers to an almost unbearable certainty and brilliance. Then, without warning, all strain was over.

The motor wound tight in him suddenly shifted to a higher gear, a gear in which its power was more than sufficient and its speed was limitless. He seemed almost to float because of the new power of perception and thought he controlled.

He glanced about him. The control room of the *Fighting Rowboat* seemed both brighter and smaller. The three-dimensional objects within its metal walls seemed to stand out aggressively, with a sort of supersolidity. He looked back at his two companions and found that even the flying fingers of Luhon seemed to have slowed.

To Miles, they had slowed. It was not as if his perception of time had altered, but as if it had *sharpened* to an intense degree. He was able to observe leisurely in one second what it might once have taken him sixty seconds to observe. But he was aware that literal time had not lengthened. Instead, it was as if his perception of it had become microscopic, so that now he could see sixty smaller divisions within the second and make as much use of each of these as he had been able to make of the whole second before.

At the same time, his imagination and understanding went soaring. In one great sweeping rush, they integrated him with the rest of the crew aboard the *Fighting Rowboat*, rushing in self-intoxicated fury upon the death that was the multitudinous enemy of the Silver Horde, with the Battle Line that had been, with the Center Aliens who had set it up—with all and everything in time past and time present, from the historic moment in which the Horde had passed through the galaxy once before up through the coming of the aliens to Earth and the present moment.

In that creative moment of understanding he achieved an understanding of it all: overdrive, his fellow crew members, the Center Aliens, everything. It was as if a man might stretch out his arms to encircle a whole universe and lock his fingers together on its farther side. It was an understanding too big for one single concept of explanation. It was a whole network of comprehensions working together.

"Join up!" he shouted into the intercom of the ship. At the same moment, he opened a channel for the overdrive power that was now in him into the network of sensitivity that encompassed them all. It flooded forth.

And the other twenty-two members of the crew felt, recognized, and absorbed it.

Like flame racing along lines of high-octane fuel, the fire

of his overdrive power flashed out and kindled overdrive fires in the awarenesses of his crewmates. Like him, they flared with a new, fierce heat, and the fire spread from them to their weapons. Like sun-dried driftwood, the psychic elements of their weapons took flame.

And from those weapons the fire reached forth in the shape of a many-times-multiplied psychic strength to capture and paralyze the new wave of the enemy now closing about them.

Miles felt it through the network of their composite sensitivity aboard the *Fighting Rowboat*—like the sudden tautening of a heavy cable mooring some massive ship to a dock. It tautened and held. Their globe of psychic force was secure. It reached out well beyond the extreme range of the weapons aboard the ships of the Silver Horde that now flocked toward it, holding all the enemy within its perimeter, helpless while the physical weapons of the tiny *Fighting Rowboat* tore at and destroyed them, one by one.

A wild joy swept them all. Here, where they should have been destroyed themselves, they were winning. For a moment it seemed to them all that they were invincible, that they could hold off and destroy the whole Silver Horde by themselves. But then the steadily mounting pressure against their psychic hold, as more and more of the silver vessels drove in on them, brought them to a more sober understanding.

As long as they could keep their present strength, they were invincible. As the Center Alien had explained to Miles earlier, the ships of the Battle Line could not be touched by the physical weapons of the enemy as long as their psychic strength endured. But either weariness or too many of the enemy pressing in on them at once could end that strength. For the moment they were winning. But they could not win forever. . . .

"Never mind that!" shouted Miles over the intercom. "We're *winning*! That's what counts! Keep it up. We're stopping the Horde—*we're stopping the Horde!*"

They fought on. The fire of their overdrive burned seemingly unquenchable under the increasing attack, like the unquenchable flame of a welding torch, burning even underwater. But that flame was consuming the reserves of strength in their minds and bodies like a potent chemical stimulant that pushed tiredness away for a while, but only at the expense of exhausting bodily reserves that should not ordinarily be tapped.

Time passed. They fought and slew the Silver Horde.
. . .

But the end was in sight now. They were not yet weakening, but the larger scout ships and even some of the light-cruiser-class ships of the Horde were beginning to push against their globe of psychic combination. Aboard the *Fighting Rowboat*, they were still many times more powerful than they should have been. But they were like a giant of a man holding shut a door against the onslaught of an avalanche. At first he holds the door shut easily against the onslaught of the rocks and boulders, but gradually these begin to pile up their weight against his shield. Heaver and heavier—until the whole weight of the mountain begans to lean against him. And against a mountain no flesh and blood can stand.

So Miles and all those aboard the *Fighting Rowboat* felt the breaking point near. Any moment now the final element of pressure would be added, their shield would crumble, and all at once the force of ten thousand weapons of the invaders would tear the little *Fighting Rowboat* to nothingness. But there was no sadness in them. Instead there was a sort of deep-lying, grim joy, like the joy of a wolf who goes down in his last fight with his jaws still locked around the throat of his enemy.

"Hold on," muttered Miles, to himself as much as to the other twenty-two he addressed over the ship's intercom. "Hold on. Keep holding a little longer—"

Sudden and thunderous, roaring without warning at them not only from the speaker in front of Miles, but from every metal strut and metal surface of the ship, unexpectedly came the voice of a Center Alien.

"Get back!" it roared. "Back to your place in the Battle Line! We're taking over the fight now!"

Miles was not conscious of having touched the communication controls before him. But suddenly on the screen there was no longer the image of the many silver ships of the Horde pressing in on them.

Instead, he saw a larger view of the battle. The little

pocket of inviolate space that the *Fighting Rowboat* had maintained around herself was now only part of a larger scene in which the front line of the Horde swirled, boiled, and retreated before the advance of a line of different ships. It was the great globular dreadnoughts of the Center Aliens and their allies came at last, after all, into the battle.

15

"Back!" roared the communications speaker. "Back to your place in the Battle Line—"

The great round, planetary shape of the nearest dreadnought was shouldering before the *Fighting Rowboat* now, obscuring three-quarters of the view of the Horde in the screen before Miles. But it was already too late. Even as the voice blared at them through the communications speaker, some mighty blow struck the tiny vessel with irresistible force—and it seemed to Miles that he went flying sideways off into nothingness.

He came back to consciousness gradually, but with a strange determination and effort, like a miner who had been trapped by a rockfall, and picking his way back to freedom, seeing the first small gleam of daylight as the last rock sealing him in tumbled aside.

From that first gleam of mental daylight, Miles swiftly returned to awareness. He found himself seated in his chair before the control console, in a *Fighting Rowboat* that felt strangely still and peaceful. In fact, through the skin of the ship itself, with that sensitivity that had come on him with overdrive during the attack, Miles knew the little ship lay once more on her platform back where it had all started.

With that realization, he switched his attention to observing the silent control room about him. The room and the motionless figures of Eff and Luhon were absolutely still. But, he discovered, so was he. His mind might be awake, but his body was asleep.

Understanding suddenly, a silent chuckle formed in the back of his mind. He recognized his condition now. He was in the grip of that same tranquilizing power which had ended all fights aboard the *Fighting Rowboat* before the Horde appeared. The only difference between the occasions when it had held him before and the present one was the fact that on mental overdrive he was apparently able to keep the sedative effects from the thought centers of his brain.

Examining himself more closely, he observed that the tranquilizing effect rolled like thick fog around the conscious center of his mind but could not enter, because of the fierce flame of his desire to be conscious which tore the fog to tatters. At the touch of that overdrive fire in him the tranquilizing fog was evaporated, so that his consciousness occupied a little clear spot, like the clear spot surrounding a hunter crouched by his morning fire in a mist-choked swamp.

Weighing the situation, Miles suspected that he could even free his physical body and have freedom of movement. And this was interesting—for he had some time since decided that the tranquilizing effect was only another version of the psychic weapon used to paralyze the Horde. Clearly, it was possible that, in overdrive and with some practice and effort, he might even be able to defy the psychic weapon himself.

But there was no point in making the effort to test his powers now. He turned his attention back to the reason for his being under tranquilization.

He freed his neck and eyes enough to be able to look down at his body. He saw that he had been stripped of nearly all his clothing. On the arms, legs, and body now revealed he saw several wounds, already closed. Only two wounds on his leg were still open—and even these were not bleeding. They seemed to be held by some invisible, interior bandage. As he watched, one of them slowly closed from the bottom upward—as if an invisible zipper were being drawn up the length of the slash. A moment later his other cut closed as well. Clearly, some unseen mechanism was at work "repairing" him, but his conscious mind took note that the curious part of it all was that this healing process, while directed from the outside, seemed to be effected by the natural responses of his own body.

He looked about the rest of the room. Eff and Luhon were also stripped and in the process of being healed. The room itself was damaged—but in a strange way. There were no holes in the walls—either of the hull or of the partitions within the ship that made up the walls and ceiling of the control room. But here and there these metal inner surfaces had flaked off in jagged shards less than two inches thick at their centers but with knifelike edges.

His brilliantly burning mind jumped immediately to an understanding. Of course—whatever weapon the Horde used would be designed for the end purpose of the Horde. It would want to kill the edible bodies of its enemies, but without rendering them inedible or spilling them out of their ships to be lost in the dark vastness of interstellar space.

Miles looked back at the vision screen before him.

There he saw the full panorama of the battle still in progress. The glittering, new-moon image of the silver invading fleet, and the hornlike tips of its line curving forward and inward, had now changed shape. Those curving arms had now swung further inward, to enclose the attacking ships of the Battle Line.

Once more Miles was reminded of the image of a monstrous amoeba attempting to engulf and absorb some edible morsel. Just so, the silver fleet had gathered into itself the globe-shaped battle formation of the ships of the Battle Line. Around that globe the ships of the Horde were now swarming, enclosing the galaxy's ships completely. What Miles viewed now was a roughly oval shape with a large bulge in the middle.

Miles looked at the battle, which, because of its vastness of scale, both in the number of ships engaged and in the amount of space they occupied, seemed on the screen to be taking place in slow motion. In slow motion and on a microscopic, rather than a telescopic, scale, for all the light-years of distance involved and the thousands-of-miles-per-second velocities of the individual ships. Suddenly there exploded in Miles a fierce hunger to know how it was going—the battle as seen by the Center Aliens and the others within that globe of space, now covered thickly and hidden from him by the swarming silver ships of the Horde.

The hunger gave birth to the means. Immediately the fiercely burning energy of overdrive within him seemed to light up one small corner of his awareness, and he discovered there a tendril of feeling, a connection with the network of sensitivity which was now in existence out there in the midst of the boiling fleet of Silver Horde vessels.

He seized on that trace and followed it. It grew as he searched along it—and suddenly he found what he hunted. He was locked, emotionally and mentally, into the network of sensitivity which joined together the ships and crews of all those in the Battle Line.

His point of view was central. It seemed to him that he existed at the very center of that vast globe of interior space held by the ships of the galaxy. Here there was no light at all, but in his mind's eye he saw it all as if everything were brightly lit—as if he stood at the center of a sun which illuminated everything.

Around him was space. Beyond this was an invisible globular shell of defensive power, held together by points spaced regularly about its surface—points which were the ships of the Battle Line. Beyond this shell for a depth of several thousand miles were helpless ships of the Horde, in a thick layer—their vessels only a few miles apart, so great was the density. Aboard those invader ships was silence. Their crews were paralyzed and still, held helpless by the psychic force and awaiting the busy scythes of the powerful physical weapons projecting from the Battle Line ships. These weapons were sweeping back and forth like search-lights, to explode—almost to disintegrate—every solid object they touched.

Outside this shell of helpless invader ships was the rest of the Silver Horde, pressing inward, trying desperately to overload the psychic mass potential of the Battle Line fleet. As Miles watched, that pressure grew until it threatened to overload the Battle Line fleet and tear apart not only the buffer-zone layer of helpless Horde ships, but also the formation of Battle Line ships beneath.

But just as overload threatened, an order pulsed outward over the network of sensitivity from whatever vessel or group of vessels among the Center Aliens commanded the rest. Abruptly the shell of defended space shrank. Suddenly the Battle Line ships were that much closer together. The surface they defended was decreased proportionately, and the layer of helpless invader ships standing in the way of the rest of the Horde that had hoped to nose in among them was that much thicker.

With the decrease in size came a proportional increase in power. The nut that the Silver Horde was attempting to crack had become smaller but denser.

The fight went on. . . .

Still the Silver Horde pressed in on the fleet it was attempting to annihilate and absorb. Like endless numbers of grasshoppers smothering a fire with their first hungry approaching waves so that those behind could enter green fields that fire defended, the Horde kept crowding in on the englobed Battle Line fleet. The pressure mounted.

Once more, swiftly, the Battle Line fleet shrank its defended space.

Once more the Battle Line ships acquired new strength. Once more the layer of paralyzed invader ships about them was increased. Still the Horde pressed in on them. . . .

Once again they decreased their defensive area and the area of their perimeter.

Now, to the eyes of Miles' physical body seated before the vision screen of the console back aboard the *Fighting Rowboat*, the shape of the Horde was nothing but one large ball of silver maggotlike shapes completely hiding those they attacked. Anyone who had not known that the Battle Line was trapped within that seething mass, thousands of miles in diameter, must have believed that there was nothing left but the Horde itself. Or that the battle, if there had been one, was already won. Only Miles' linkage with the sensitivity network allowed him to know that the combat still went on.

It had now reached the point of deadlock. The uncountable numbers of the Horde were jammed as tightly as they safely could be about a linked fleet of Battle Line ships that had shrunk to what was its smallest practical diameter of defended space.

Like two massive organisms entangled in a motionless, straining struggle for life or death, the Battle Line and the Silver Horde clung, locked together. It was the sort of straining deadlock which, between human wrestlers, could not have existed for more than a matter of minutes without one opponent or the other giving way in exhaustion. But so massive were the antagonists wrapped in their death struggle beyond the spiral arm of the galaxy that this deadlock continued not for minutes but for hours. And for hours—which seemed like minutes—Miles endured with it, while around him Eff, Luhon, and the others returned to consciousness and began to move around the *Fighting Rowboat*.

They did not speak to Miles. Just as his sensitivity continued linking him with the network of the encompassed Battle Line, so their sensitivity to him had continued. They were aware that he was somehow *with* the battle out there on their screens in a way that they could not be. So they moved about him silently and left him in silence to endure with those who still fought on, hidden by the Horde.

Miles was only peripherally aware of his crewmates. Almost all his awareness was concentrated on the network of sensitivity of the embattled ships. About their globe the Silver Horde was still clustered—and the deadlock continued as if it would never break.

Then, abruptly, it broke.

Suddenly the physical eyes of Miles, watching in the vision screen aboard the *Fighting Rowboat*, saw something that must have begun to happen some moments before but which was now becoming apparent. The Horde swarm enclosing the ships of the Battle Line was no longer globe-shaped. Instead, it was beginning to bulge at one end, becoming faintly pear-shaped. Now, as Miles concentrated his attention on that bulging end, he saw that the bulge was growing, was stretching out—was, in fact, pulling off from the mass surrounding the ships of the Battle Line. Now, as he watched with a perception that speeded up the slow motion imposed on the battle action by the vast units of time and space involved, the bulge began to thin out to a point, stretching away from the fighting ships of the galaxy and away from the galaxy itself.

Slowly the line of fleeing invader ships lengthened and thickened. The awareness of their retreat pulsed through Miles back into the sensitivity network of the still-enclosed Battle Line, and the knowledge was received there like a trumpet call of victory—but the fight went on.

Because, for the englobed ships of the Battle Line, the battle was not yet over. Those silver ships still just without the layer of paralyzed invader vessels continued to fight blindly to move in and overwhelm the defenders. It would be long hours yet—perhaps several days—before the Battle Line dared break its defensive formation.

But outside, as seen on the vision screen of the *Fighting Rowboat,* the shifting shape of the invading fleet continued to lengthen and withdraw, pulling away from its engagement with the Battle Line and forming a new sickle shape headed away from the galaxy.

The invaders had been turned from their feeding ground. The Silver Horde, which no one had been able to stop a million years ago, had now been stopped and averted from its goal. The galaxy, the stars of home, the Earth itself were saved.

16

There was no darkness aboard the egg-shaped craft that was transporting all twenty-three of the *Fighting Rowboat*'s crew to the command ship of the Center Aliens, but Miles had the feeling that if it had been dark, Luhon's eyes would have glowed in the obscurity like the fierce eyes of a cat in the night.

"We shamed them into it!" Luhon said almost in a whisper in Miles' ear. "When we talk to them, friend Miles, remember that! They'd decided to run, but when we attacked, we shamed them into coming back to fight!"

Miles said nothing. Within him was an awareness that both the problem and its resolution had been wider and deeper than Luhon or any of the others understood. But there was no time for him to explain this to them. Luhon's words still echoed in his ear even as the gray ship transporting them seemed to melt away, and they found themselves apparently hanging in space at the midpoint of the interior of one of the huge Center Alien vessels.

They hung or stood there like bodies at a point where gravity balanced in all directions. It was a little like being in a fun house full of distorting mirrors. For looking about casually, Miles could see that they were literally miles in every direction from the interior surface of the globe shape surrounding them. They were too far away to make out the fact of what was abnormally and immediately apparent to them—that the whole interior surface of this globe was filled with individuals of the Center Alien race and their allies. It was as if an auditorium were to be built in the shape of some huge ball, with seats completely covering its inner surface.

When Miles glanced generally at the interior of the globe surrounding him, he saw only a blurred grayness in the far distance, illuminated by a light that seemed to be nowhere in particular but filling all the interior space equally. However, when he looked directly at any one spot on the interior globe face, it was as if some telescopic window had suddenly materialized between him and that point. All at once he was staring into the faces of the aliens seated or standing there, as if no more than ten or a dozen feet separated them from him.

Clearly, this gathering was in honor of the crew of the *Fighting Rowboat*. But, clearly also, the occasion was something more than a mere celebration. Miles felt, with his new sensitivity, a puzzlement reaching out toward them from the surrounding audience. He and his crewmates were being viewed with a strange curiosity and no little lack of understanding.

Suddenly they were joined at their midpoint position by two of the Center Aliens. To Miles' eyes, these still wore human forms. But he was understanding enough now to realize that while he saw them in this fashion, Luhon would be seeing them with the shape and features of Luhon's race—and so on, individually and differently with each one of the rest of the crew.

Miles reached back into his own mind for support, and the now-familiar overdrive reaction abruptly flowed through him, making his vision sharp and clear. Deductions clicked in his mind like totals on an efficient adding machine. The two Center Aliens who had appeared looked no different than all the others he had seen, but the deductive section of his mind told him that they must be different. These two would not have been chosen at random to stand and talk to the crew of the *Fighting Rowboat* before the eyes of the—was it hundreds of thousands or millions?—that occupied the inner surface of the globe, watching them. No, it was more likely—in fact, it was almost a certainty—that these two were as close to being the supreme authorities among the Center Aliens as any of that race available here and now.

A nudge of Luhon's elbow against Miles' rib reminded him of the other side of the equation. Luhon was waiting for Miles to speak, because Miles was their leader aboard the *Fighting Rowboat*. But Luhon, like the rest, was fiercely expecting that Miles would charge the Center Aliens with cowardice. The gray-skinned alien was waiting for Miles to remind the Center Aliens that they had fled the Battle Line, had run, and that the battle would have been lost if it had not been for the suicidal wild attack of the *Fighting Rowboat*.

Miles, through a mind that was as clear as a perfect lens held up to a powerful light, saw himself caught between the points of view of two groups, neither of which really understood what had happened.

"We have brought you here to do you honor," said the taller of the two Center Aliens. Deductively, for all the lack of variance of feature in this one, as in the others of his race, Miles judged him to be old—probably very old. Once more Luhon's elbow bored sharply into Miles' side.

"Thank you," said Miles. "We appreciate the fact that you want to honor us. But there's a question we want to ask you—all of you."

"Ask anything you wish," replied the Center Alien, and Miles could feel the millions of individual minds all around them, as if the distance at which they were was at once hundreds of miles and only a few feet away, focusing their attention on him and on the question to come.

"Why did you come back?" Miles asked. "You told us that there was no hope of winning the battle. But after we attacked alone, it seems you changed your minds. Of course, we all know the results. The Silver Horde was driven off. But what are we supposed to think about your actions, first running and then returning? Were you wrong in your first judgment of how the battle would go? Or did the sight of us attacking alone make you more aware of your own responsibilities to stand and fight?"

There was no immediate answer to Miles' question. The two Center Aliens stood looking at him as if they were consulting silently with the uncountable numbers that surrounded them, watching. Finally, the taller one spoke again.

"Forgive me," said the Center Alien, "if I seem to insult

you by mentioning once more your barbarian condition. But if you were not so primitive and emotion-driven, you would have understood by now why we came back. The fault is ours, of course, being the older and more capable people, for not realizing you had not understood."

"Then perhaps you'll explain it now," said Miles.

"Of course," said the Center Alien. "May I remind you that it was not an organic decision—our conclusion that our joining battle with the Silver Horde could only result in our defeat? It was a computed decision, the logical result of many factors considered and handled by nonliving devices which are far superior to the aggregate decision-making possibilities of even *our* minds. The factors of the situation were made available continually to these computational devices. At Decision Point, their assessment was plain. The Horde had a tiny but undeniable edge in the total of probability factors needed for victory. We could not logically hope to fight them and win. Therefore, we made the only sensible alternative decision: that all those within the Battle Line should flee and attempt to save themselves as well as possible, in order to have the largest possible number of intelligent, technologically trained individuals with which to rebuild the galaxy after the Horde had passed."

"But you changed your minds," said Miles.

"No," answered the Center Alien. "We are advanced beyond the point where we could, as you say, change our minds—make an emotional judgment at variance with the results of our computations. We came back, not because we 'changed our minds,' but because new computations gave us a different answer."

"New computations?" demanded Miles.

"Of course," replied the Center Alien quietly. "I imagine even you can understand that by attacking as you did, you could introduce a change into the factors on which a judgment of the battle's outcome had been figured. Three matters of sheer chance affected the present situation and altered the future picture built on that situation. First, there was the fact that you had suicidally, and against all reason, chosen to attack alone against the total might of the Horde. Second, there was the fact that your attack came from what had been the farthest end of our Battle

146

Line. Third, there was the fact that reacting with the instinct of their race, the total fleet of the Silver Horde began to turn to meet your attack instead of ignoring it and allowing it to be abosrbed, and yourselves obliterated, by the smallest fraction of its number necessary to deal with you. These things, as I say, altered the factors of the situation. Now I am sure you understand."

Beside Miles, Luhon's elbow no longer urged him on. With his sensitivity, Miles could feel the other crew members, behind him, baffled but equally spellbound.

"Perhaps. But explain it to me anyway," said Miles.

"If you wish. You have earned whatever explanation you desire," said the Center Alien. "As I said, your illogical, suicidal attack altered the factors of the situation—not only to our view, but evidently to the Horde's as well. Your attack, alone, must have been something they could not understand, so that they expected the worst and turned their full strength to crush you. Our devices recomputed and found, as a result, that where before the slight but decisive edge of advantage had been in favor of the Horde, now because of your action there was an equally slight but decisive edge of advantage in our favor."

The Center Alien paused. Miles could feel all the eyes within that huge globe on him and his companions.

"So," the Center Alien went on with the same unvarying tone of voice, as if he were discussing something of no more importance than the time of day, "we came back and engaged the Horde after all."

For a moment, within Miles' brilliantly burning mind, a faint flicker of guilt awoke. With an ability to understand that he would not have had if he had not been in overdrive, he read clearly and sharply some of the meanings behind the Center Alien's words. The individuals of this race, for all their lack of apparent emotion, wanted to live as badly as he did. Also, while their decisions were governed by their computing devices, they had no means of knowing whether that computation was ultimately correct or not. They had only known that the answer they got was the best that could be gotten within their power and the power of their computers. So, just as they had fled without shame—but undoubtedly with as deep an inner pain at the thought of what they were doing in abandoning their

147

worlds to the onslaught of the Horde—they had returned without question. The had returned with as deep an inner courage as was possible to them, to enter a battle which they could not be sure they would win.

Miles felt Luhon stir against him. There was a quality of indecisiveness in that movement that announced that the gray-skinned crewmate was cut adrift from his earlier fierce desire to make the Center Aliens admit to cowardice. Now it was plain they could not be taken to task at all in the sense that Luhon and the others had envisioned. For they had done nothing, after all, but be true to their own different pattern of behavior.

"Thank you," said Miles. "Now we understand."

"We are glad you understand," said the taller Center Alien. "But since this is a moment for understanding, there is something we would like to ask you."

"Ask away," said Miles, already expecting what was to come.

"Of all who joined us in the Battle Line," said the Center Alien, "you twenty-three were the only ones who did not obey our order to retreat and save yourselves. Instead, you did a clearly reasonless thing. You attacked the Silver Horde alone. Yet all of you are thinking beings, though primitive. You must have realized that nothing you could do would make any difference to the question of whether your native worlds and peoples would escape or survive the Horde once it was among the stars of our galaxy. Also, you must have known that by no miracle whatsoever could your one tiny ship so much as slow down the advance of the Horde for a moment. In short, you knew that attacking them could do no good, that it was only a throwing away of your own lives. Older and many times advanced over you as we are, we should understand why you would do such a thing. But we do not. Alone, with no hope, why did you attack the Horde the way you did? Was there some way you could guess that by attacking, you would bring the rest of us back to join you in fighting after all?"

It struck Miles then, with the clarity of his overdrive-sharpened mind, that this was the first time he had ever heard one of the Center Alien race ask a question. Obviously this could mean only one thing. It must have occurred to this advanced race that the only reasonable possibility was that Miles and the others had some means of calculating the battle odds within their own minds and bodies which was superior to the calculating devices the Center Aliens themselves used.

"No," answered Miles. "We didn't expect you back. We knew we were attacking the Horde on our own, and we knew what had to happen if we met them alone."

"Yes," said the Center Alien. There was a second of silence. Then he went on—to Miles' extrasensive perceptions, it seemed, a little heavily. "We were almost certain that you could not have expected help. But, seeing you did not expect help, the question remains of why you did it."

"We had no choice," said Miles.

"No choice?" The Center Alien stared strangely at him. "You had a clear choice. Your choice was to leave, as you had been ordered to do."

"No," said Miles.

Once more he was conscious of standing between two points of view: the point of view of the Center Aliens and that of his crewmates—neither of whom fully saw and understood the situation and what had taken place in their meeting with the Horde. It was up to Miles now to satisfy them both, even if he could make neither understand what he now understood.

"Maybe it's because, as you say, we're primitive compared to the rest of you in the Battle Line," said Miles slowly. "But our choice wasn't a head choice, it was a heart choice. I don't believe I can explain it to you. I can only tell you that it's that way—with us. You can't take people like myself and those here with me, who care for their own races, and set them out between those races and an enemy who threatens utter destruction—and then expect that we whom you set there will be able to step aside, leaving our people unshielded, simply because logic dictates that we're going to lose if we try to fight the destroyer."

He paused. From the beginning the huge globeful of watchers had been silent, and there was no more silence now than there had been before. Yet Miles felt a certain extra focusing of attention on him, a metaphorical holding of the breath by the hundreds of thousands or millions who were listening. He went on.

149

"Probably," he said, "there's no way for me to make you understand this. But in running away without fighting the Horde, we were leaving our people—probably to die. And we couldn't do that. We aren't built that way—so that we can cold-bloodedly save ourselves if they're likely to be wiped out. To save ourselves under those conditions would have required a self-control greater than any of us has."

Once more he paused. The globeful of listeners still listened.

"Our peoples," Miles said, slowly, "are part of us, you see—the way our arms and legs are parts of our body. We couldn't any more abandon them just to save ourselves than we could coolly submit to cutting off all our arms and legs so that the useless trunks of our bodies would be left to survive. If our people had to face death, the least we could do—not the most, but the *least*—was to face that death with them. It wasn't any thinking decision we made. I repeat, it was an instinctive decision—to kill as many of the Horde as we could before we were killed. It wasn't any different for us than if we'd come back and found our planets turned to desert, our people dead—and *then* we'd run into the Horde. Then, just as we did here, we'd have tried without thinking to kill as many of the Horde as we could before we were killed ourselves."

Miles stopped talking. The silence that followed his words this time was a long one. But at last it was broken by the taller of the two aliens standing with the crew of the *Fighting Rowboat* at midpoint.

"We were right originally then," said the Center Alien slowly. "It was a part of your primitive nature that caused it—and we could not understand, because it is a part we have long abandoned. You are still on that early road from which we departed a very long time ago. Do not think, though, that we are less grateful to you because of what you have just told us."

He turned a little so that his gaze was directly on Miles. The Center Alien seemed almost to speak directly and privately to Miles.

"No matter from what source it sprang," said the Center Alien, "from will or mind or instinct, the fact remains that what you did changed the battle picture and resulted in our

150

saving our galaxy. What can we do for you and these others to show our gratitude?"

Miles had been prepared for the question. Now he answered quickly before any of the others from the *Fighting Rowboat* could speak up.

"We want to stay independent," said Miles, "and much of what you could give us might not be good for that independence. But there are a few things. . . . Now that we've been brought together aboard the *Fighting Rowboat*, we'd like our races to stay in touch. So give us ships then, or show us how to build our own ships, so that our twenty-three different races can communicate and travel among our separate worlds."

"The ships and the knowledge you ask for are yours," said the Center Alien. He hesitated. "And if in the future you should want more than this from us, we will arrange a method of communication so that you need only ask."

"Thanks," said Miles. "But I don't think we'll be asking."

17

The summer sun of a later year was sinking toward the hours of late afternoon above the high banks of the Mississippi River by the University of Minnesota campus when the envoy from that race called (by themselves) the *Rahsesh* alighted from a government car at the edge of a road on the west bank of the river. Before the envoy, humans in plain clothes guarded a small section of green lawn that ran outward a short distance to the edge of a bluff. Recognized by the guards, in his personal and diplomatic capacities, the alien envoy was admitted through their lines. He went alone across the grass to where a man stood with his back turned, painting on a large canvas set up on a heavy easel. A brown-haired girl sat quietly in a camp chair near him, reading.

The painter was in light slacks and white shirt with sleeves rolled up. Smears of gray, blue, and yellow paint were on his bared forearms, on his hands and fingers, and the canvas before him was heavy with wet paint of many colors. The envoy from the *Rahsesh* went swiftly, smoothly, and quietly up to stand at his elbow.

"Am I interrupting you, friend Miles?" he asked the painter.

"No," Miles shook his head without looking around. "I'm all done, Luhon. I'm just putting a little polish on a last few sections. You've met my wife, Marie?"

She raised her head to smile at Luhon before returning to her book.

"No. I'm honored to meet her," said Luhon. "Continue with your occupation, friend Miles. I can wait."

"No, go ahead. Talk," said Miles, still without turning. "Do you know you're the first one in? None of the rest of our old crew from the *Fighting Rowboat* has got to Earth yet."

"They'll be along shortly, I'd guess," said Luhon. "Did each of the races pick its former representative to be its envoy? It occurred to me that there might be races which might want to send someone else."

"Not for this meeting," said Miles. His brush point placed yellow color lightly on the canvas. "Each of our twenty-three races needs all the understanding it can get about the others, and that sort of understanding is possible only through someone who already knows the rest of us. In fact, I said as much in the message I sent around to the other races. You must have noticed my recommendation to that effect in the letter I sent the *Rahsesh*."

"I noticed," replied Luhon, gazing at the canvas with some small interest and curiosity. "But it occurred to me that perhaps the recommendation was special in my case."

"No," said Miles.

For a few seconds neither one said anything. Miles worked away at his painting.

"You know, friend Miles," said Luhon thoughtfully, "when the Center Aliens asked you, after the battle with the Silver Horde, what we all wanted in the way of reward, you answered him without talking it over with the rest of us first."

"That's right," answered Miles, painting.

"And now," murmured Luhon, "here you've called a meeting of all of us on your world, speaking for all our races—again all on your own. Also, that notice you sent around, friend Miles, didn't say especially what we all were getting together to discuss."

"It said," said Miles, "that what we were going to discuss would at first be understandable only to those who, like we twenty-three, had had experience with the Center Aliens and the Silver Horde."

"True," said Luhon, "and that was enough to satisfy my government—and, I suppose, those who govern the other twenty-one races. But is it going to be satisfactory to the twenty-three of us, when we all come face to face again, I ask you, friend Miles?"

"All right. You've asked me," answered Miles, and paused to squint at the descending sun sending its rays slanting now across university buildings, trees, river bluffs, and river—the entire scene of Miles' painting. "And you've made a point of coming early, to be sure that you'd be the first to ask me."

"I was your second-in-command," Luhon reminded him mildly.

"True," said Miles, straightening up and stepping back from the canvas, brush in hand, to get a longer perspective at what he was doing. "All right, friend Luhon. I'll give you your answer. I've called us all together again here to begin making plans for the day when it'll be our turn, eventually, to take over control of the galaxy from the Center Aliens."

His words sounded calmly on the warm summer air. But they were received by Luhon in a silence that stretched out and out.

Miles went on, unperturbed, examining his canvas. He stepped forward once more and began to make a few more tiny alterations on it with the yellow-tipped number ten brush he still held. Finally, behind him, Luhon spoke again.

"I have my people to think of," said Luhon slowly. "If you've become mentally unreliable, friend Miles, I'll put off whatever friendship and allegiance I had to you and so inform the rest of the twenty-two—crewmates and races alike."

"That's up to you," said Miles. "Meanwhile, why don't you think a little about what I've just said? I didn't say anything about taking over from the Center Aliens tomorrow, or next year, or even a thousand years from now. I said that we'd be taking over eventually—and we needed to start talking about that eventuality now."

"Have you forgotten"—Luhon's voice was almost a whisper—"the number of Center Alien ships in the Battle Line? Have you forgotten the number of Center Aliens that each of those great ships must have held? And what *one* Center Alien was able to do to our whole ship and crew? Can you imagine how many like him there must be, and the number of worlds they must occupy, in toward the galaxy's center? Can you imagine all that and the thousands of years of technological advantage they must have over us—and still say what you're saying?"

"That's right. I can," said Miles flatly, putting his brush away finally into a jar of muddy turpentine standing on a small table to the left of his easel. "Because it isn't numbers or technology that're the true measure of a race. We found that out when the Horde attacked."

"Did we, friend Miles?" Luhon's eyes narrowed to dark lines in his gray face.

"I'm reminding you," said Miles, "that the Center Aliens failed the rest of the galaxy in the moment of the attack of the Horde. I didn't think you'd forget that."

"Forget? No," replied Luhon slowly. His eyes widened once more.

"Think!" said Miles, turning for the first time to face him. "Nothing shrinks faster with time than the memory of a great struggle. Right now, my race has been completely shaken up, awakened, by its escape from the Horde. But the generation remembering this, the one that shared consciousness with me out there on the Battle Line, isn't going to live forever. How much will its grandchildren remember?"

He paused, staring at Luhon.

"Not—not much," said Luhon, hesitantly. "If your people are like mine, forgetfulness will take the edge off memory, in time. That's true. . . ."

"Of course it's true!" said Miles. "In a hundred years they'll start forgetting that we didn't really conquer the Horde—only caused it enough trouble so that it turned aside to easier feeding grounds. In a thousand years they'll talk about the great victory we won. In two thousand, it'll have been an easy and expected victory. Soon—very soon—as the whole galaxy figures time, another million years'll have gone by and the Horde will be back again. And how ready will we be?"

Luhon hesitated.

"Very well," he said after a second. "But why us? Why not leave the control and the responsibility of remembering to the Center Aliens—or whoever takes their place down in the middle of the galaxy? They kept the records of the Horde's coming once before."

"Kept the records, yes," said Miles. He looked down from his slightly greater height at the gray-skinned alien. "But that's all they did. Millions of years ago, remember, the Horde wasn't stopped at all. It swept through this galaxy, almost emptying it of life. The Center Aliens must have been one of the few technological races of which individuals survived. But in spite of that, this time the Horde would have done exactly the same thing it did before—if it hadn't been for us. Us! We twenty-three aboard the *Fighting Rowboat*!"

"You have to admit," said Luhon, quietly, "luck had a lot to do with it—with all we did."

"No," said Miles, "I don't have to admit that. Because it wasn't luck. It was something much more important than luck—and that something's to be the topic of this meeting I've called. Because we've got it—a hope and a power that the Center Aliens haven't, and that's why they failed, facing the Horde."

"Failed?" Luhon's voice was almost too quiet.

"They ran. We stayed—and saved the day," said Miles. "Because of our blind instincts, but also because of something I'd found and shared with the rest of you. The ability to go into an overdrive state, to tap hysterical strength of the mind and body. Only 'hysterical strength' is really the wrong term for it. Because what it is, actually, is a breakthrough into a creative ability to draw on all the deepest reservoirs of our minds and bodies at once. Remember how you felt when we attacked the Horde and I reached out to all of you with the strength that was in me?"

155

"I remember," said Luhon.

"Then you remember that the Center Aliens didn't have anything like that in themselves. If they had, we'd have felt it. More than that, they'd never have needed to run from the Horde in the first place, if their naturally greater psychic strength could be multipled as ours into overdrive."

"Unmultiplied, their strength was enough—once they did come back and start fighting," said Luhon.

"Yes, once they came back!" said Miles. "But the point is, they didn't come. Not until after we, with no hope, just instinct, had attacked the Horde and changed the battle odds for them. The odds meant everything to them— nothing else did."

"Friend Miles," murmured Luhon, "it seems to me you make too much of one small difference."

"It's not just the difference," replied Miles more quietly. "It's what the difference tells me about the Center Aliens. Don't you remember how they didn't understand—even after I'd explained it—why we aboard the *Fighting Rowboat* felt we'd no choice but to attack the Silver Horde, even though we were left alone? Remember how that was something that the Center Aliens couldn't get?"

"They'd changed, over their longer period of civilization," said Luhon. "They explained that."

"Changed, yes!" said Miles almost fiercely. "*They'd* changed—so that they couldn't any longer understand our reacting the way we did. But it was still *our* reaction that triggered off their own fight to save the galaxy, and that fight succeeded in spite of all their earlier calculations! Don't you see? They'd given up their instincts, years ago, for what they thought were other advantages. But those other advantages couldn't save them—and our instincts, filling in where theirs were missing, did!"

"All this," said Luhon, "I admit, friend Miles. Maybe we do have something the Center Aliens gave up, and maybe their lack of it would have opened the galaxy to the Silver Horde if we hadn't been there. But how can you make this one small, instinctive reaction a basis for some sweeping plan to replace the lords of our island universe?"

Miles smiled a little grimly. He picked up a clean piece

of white cloth from the small table, soaked it in kerosene from a container standing nearby, and began to clean the red, the gray, the yellow paint from his hands and lower arms.

"Because it isn't small," he said. "You, I—all of us on the *Fighting Rowboat*—made a wrong guess about the Center Aliens from the start. Seeing how old and powerful they were, we took it for granted that they'd long ago won all their battles with their environment, that they'd evolved beyond the point where they had to prove their right to survive in the universe. But we were wrong."

Luhon looked strangely at Miles.

"I don't understand you," the gray-skinned alien said.

"I'll explain," said Miles. He finished cleaning his hands and, wadding up the now sodden and stained piece of white cloth, threw it into a large coffee can half-filled with other paint-soaked rags.

"Somewhere," he said, "sometime, there may be an end to the physical universe. But only then—only when there are no more frontiers over which something unknown and inimical can come to attack—is any race's struggle for survival going to be over. Up until then, each race is going to have to keep on proving itself. The only differences are going to be that the challenges to survival will come from farther and farther away, as it expands the area it's made safe for itself to live in. We humans, Luhon, are end products of an organism that started as a one-celled animal and that, to date, has won every battle for life that's been forced on it. How is it with your people?"

"The same," murmured Luhon. "But surely the Center Aliens also—"

"No," said Miles. "Somewhere, back thousands of years probably, they made the decision to scrap their instincts for other abilities. And for all those thousands of years it looked like the right decision. Then the Silver Horde came back and proved it was wrong. Oh, the Center Aliens survived the Horde physically, but that doesn't matter, because it was we, not they, who saved them. They were proved vulnerable—and they can't go back to pick up what they've lost. All at once, their road into the future turns out to have been a dead-end route all along."

Miles looked for a long second at Luhon.

"So that's why we'll be taking over the galaxy from them," he went on. "Because from that moment on, they'll have begun to die—somewhere in their race consciousness—just like any prehistoric species that took the wrong evolutionary road and finally came up against something it couldn't handle."

"But, friend Miles," said Luhon, "even if they do die off and we take their place, if we hold on to our instincts, how can we gain what they gained at the price of giving up their instincts? Where can we go—"

"By another route," said Miles, "any other evolutionary road where we hold on to instinct and emotion. They couldn't have given that sort of road much of a try, or they wouldn't have turned away from it so early. They closed a door to themselves that the rest of us, with luck, are going through into a much bigger universe."

"Bigger?" Luhon's tone was doubtful.

"Of course bigger," said Miles. "Take the overdrive—it's from instinct and emotion that you get into overdrive. Can you imagine getting it any other way?"

"But we can't spend all our future fighting off invaders, Miles."

Miles smiled. "Is that all you think overdrive is good for? That's the least of what it can do for you. It's a basically *creative* force—"

Miles broke off and put a friendly hand on the smooth, gray-skinned shoulder beside him.

"You'll see," Miles said. "You'll understand, once I explain it. And I'll be explaining it to all of you from the *Fighting Rowboat*, once everyone's here for the meeting." He checked himself again. "Which reminds me, we'd better be getting back to welcome the rest of them as they get here. Marie?"

She rose from her chair, her finger in her book to mark her place, and walked back toward the road.

But under Miles' hand, Luhon stood still. His attention suddenly caught and arrested, he was leaning forward, staring at the painting. Miles waited and for a moment watched the gray face, in blunt profile, staring at the shapes and colors on the stretched cloth.

Finally, Luhon sighed briefly and relaxed his attention. He turned to Miles, looking sideways and up at the taller human being.

"You've got a lot of sun in it, friend Miles," he said. "Is that—"

Miles' smile widened. He pushed the shoulder he still held, lightly, turning Luhon about, back toward the road, and they started for the car that still waited there.

"That's right," said Miles as they went. "That's overdrive, too. There in my painting, and yes—there *is* a lot of sun in it."

So they went. But in fact, Luhon was correct. For though the scene was the same as the one Miles had painted on the day—years ago, it seemed now—that the sun had turned sullen and red, there was a difference in this canvas.

Once again the painted scene showed the river, the river bluffs, the green lawns and red-brick university buildings—not as they appeared objectively, but grayed and hardened, stained with the marks of old, savage, animal guilts and primitive human failures. Once again the brush of Miles had shown the works of man sitting in grim judgment on man himself. For all his searching, his artistic vision had not been changed in that, after all.

But something new had been added.

Over the whole scene now lay a new quality of sunlight in the full value of its illumination. It filled every corner of the painting. It lay over and around the hardness and the stains, and although it did not hide them, it laid hold on and altered all the parts of the picture.

Gathered up, held, and bound by that new sunlight now, the river, bluffs, and finally, buildings—all the past and present—seemed to melt and flow together into a single soaring structure. A structure capable of being destroyed, perhaps, but never of being turned by outside force alone from its common, fierce, and instinctive striving . . . upward into the light.

THE AUTHOR

GORDON DICKSON knew at a young age he was going to be a writer. At fifteen he entered the University of Minnesota to work toward a degree in creative writing. After an interruption for military service during World War II, he continued at the university, doing graduate work after earning his Bachelor of Arts. He has been a full-time professional writer ever since. His science fiction earned him a Hugo Award in 1964 and the Nebula Award of the Science Fiction Writers of America in 1966. Mr. Dickson lives in Minneapolis.